The Knowledge Crystals

Lauren Bischoff

ISBN 979-8-88751-225-9 (paperback)
ISBN 979-8-88751-226-6 (digital)

Christian Faith Publishing
832 Park Avenue
Meadville, PA 16335
www.christianfaithpublishing.com

Printed in the United States of America

Chapter 1

Pumpkin Auken—a glamorous orange cat who had enormous green eyes and wore elegant clothing—was tending to his garden outside. The garden behind his town house had a small fence around it, which kept the rabbits from his backyard. It was very early in the morning. The sun had not yet risen above the trees, and a peaceful silver mist tickled his nose and whiskers.

"The dandelions have lost their roars," Pumpkin said as he observed that the lion-faced plants growing in a garden patch had remained silent. "I have just the thing for them."

He went into his greenhouse, where he grabbed the food he had invented. He called the plant food Roaring Seed. This was one of the things Pumpkin was famous for. He had done many wonders for the universe when it came to innovation.

Pumpkin had built a prototype for his upcoming invention, the Boot-Hoot. The prototype was a diorama of a mobile-home camper that he would design for traveling around the globe—not to mention for the dimensions of other worlds yet to be discovered.

The reason he was creating such a thing was because he had heard talk earlier in town all about an unfortunate incident that had happened to an unknown city called Atlantis. He overheard a story at the bar he went to on nights when there was a full moon. He had seen a couple of mousers sitting there at the bar last time, sharing a toast in celebration for the kingdom that once existed within the sky. They were saying the kingdom had gotten blown up and had fallen to pieces after some kind of invasion, and its magic had been drained. No one specifically knew why. However, the kingdom wasn't too good to begin with, and the search for the princess was called off.

The rest of the cats believed the princess had died along with the queen after the chaos was created. A thought then came to Pumpkin about the odd event a while ago. When was the last time he had ever spoken to his brother? He had called him ages ago, and a response should have come by now.

Maybe something came up with him, and it's why I ain't hearing anything yet, Pumpkin thought as he prepared to spray his dandelions to strengthen their energy.

The dandelions are not acting as lionish as they should while the other flowers he had were all right, like the catnips that snapped at the bugs flying past him. Pumpkin took time to observe the finest things in life with his knowledgeable eyes. "My poor babies. You are so deserving of this drink. Sorry it took so long. You must've starved."

"Pumpkin!" a super high-pitched voice came from inside his home, bringing him away from tending to his garden. He crinkled his eyebrows as the glass-stained windows surrounding him broke, and he turned to face the back door leading toward his house. Standing before the patio in his small backyard was Tigger with a huge grin on his face.

"Tigger," Pumpkin said. "I guess you have gotten my message, haven't you?"

"Yep, and I am also here for some tea and biscuits," Tigger said. He was a petite tannish cat who also had green compassionate eyes. He was wearing a detective's outfit upon entering the garden, and it looked as if he was having a complicated time getting his muddy black boots off his feet.

"Have you read the *Daily Yarn*?" Pumpkin asked.

"No, not recently. Why? What's happening?"

"Take a look at this," Pumpkin said as he showed Tigger the article from the newspaper he received this morning.

Tigger got up after taking his muddy boots off and left them on the floor. He strolled over to take an overview of the black, red, and white paper. The image upon it showed the book of crystals drained of its magic, and there was information about the kingdom's rumble with evidence of the gemstones being scattered across the universe as these crashed into other dimensions, creating chaos. There was even a number to call for anyone having any leads or information on the crystals' whereabouts.

"They're holding a prize for the one who collects and returns the crystals to the kingdom, restoring order in the other dimensions." Pumpkin continued to explain, "Ya know, I sense that we will be able to find those crystals and collect that reward. We both know that those crystals not only affect our world but also could affect other worlds, for we are all connected. What happens here can have an effect on the other realms and vice versa."

"Hmm. Ya think?"

"So what do you think? How about you and I going and getting these crystals in order to collect this reward being offered."

"Well, okay." Tigger sounded rather convinced. "It has been a while since we've been camping or traveling together. I'd love to go on an adventure."

"But how? It would take a while for me to build the Boot-Hoot. You know I just have its prototype finished, so we don't have any transportation yet."

A shout came from over the fence, "Hey, Pumpkin and Tigger, guess what?!"

Pumpkin and Tigger turned their heads to see another cat, who was midgetlike with black fur as dark as a shadow and a white chin, making him almost look like some kind of feline in a tuxedo. He was trying to peek over the backyard, which they had fenced off.

"What?" Pumpkin asked, rolling his eyes at the unwelcome nuisance of their cousin Nicky. "What is it now, Nicky?"

"You'll never believe what I have done."

"I bet not," Pumpkin grumbled as he had a seat in his chair, pouring himself a cup of tea. And he said while taking a sip, "Please do tell us what idiotic plot you've done this time."

"I took your prototype and built the Boot-Hoot," Nicky announced.

Pumpkin spat out the tea he was drinking directly into Tigger's face as he choked on the rest of the liquid, which he swallowed.

"Thanks, Pumpkin. I needed a shower." Tigger growled, patting himself dry after being spat on.

Pumpkin smiled sheepishly and said, "Sorry." And then he glanced back at Nicky with his eyes filled with a little agitation. "You what? Can you repeat that?"

"I built your Boot-Hoot invention. Want to come and see?" Nicky kept on urging the two cats. He was so full of energy and excitement. "I really finished the Boot-Hoot."

"Pumpkin…" Tigger looked his brother in the eye, his smile growing even larger as it stretched out to his ears. "It couldn't be better timing."

Pumpkin sighed. Unpleasant thoughts and images began forming inside his mind. This can't be. Nicky couldn't possibly have finished the project he'd been working on for more than a week. They rarely trusted their cousin with building any inventions, especially after Nicky had an incident with a snapping turtle, which sent him over the edge. He squinted his left eye as if he was winking, still not too trusting of his cousin's words. "Well, let's check out his work, Tigger. Let's see if it is roadworthy."

"Follow me," said Nicky.

Pumpkin and Tigger followed Nicky out front to inspect the Boot-Hoot. Their eyes widened as their cousin moved out of the way.

Pumpkin couldn't believe it. Nicky really had completed the vehicle. It was the same image he had on his blueprints. His cousin must've stolen them from him the day he accepted the award from the town square for his invention prototype of the Boot-Hoot. Here it was, the fantastic Boot-Hoot standing in one piece. Just to be sure, he walked up to the vehicle and began tapping upon it from its door to the wheels, examining every inch. There were no loose screws or minor adjustments to be made. It was created as it should be, and it was as steady as a fiddle.

"I can't find any issues," Pumpkin announced, making Tigger and Nicky sigh with relief.

"If you can't find any problems," Tigger said, walking up and placing a paw on his brother's shoulder, "does that mean we can begin packing to head out and be on our way?"

Pumpkin nodded. "We could go…" But then something came to his mind. "However, what about my garden? I can't leave it unattended."

"I will look after it while you're away." Nicky stepped up boldly. "Besides, I couldn't go with you guys anyway. You know how easily I get lost with my mind jumbling around and sending me off into tangents. I cannot control that part of myself. It's the way I am. I will screw everything up. Besides, I did my part in building the Boot-Hoot. Now it's up to you and Tigger. You both will need it, but this doesn't mean I won't be in contact. As an additional upgrade, I installed a projector screen within the thingy so you can call me from anywhere anytime in any of the other dimensions during your travels."

"That's very clever of you, Nicky. I couldn't have built this better myself," Pumpkin said. "Oh, but just one more thing. How did you know we needed this?"

"Yeah. Freaky, isn't it?" Nicky replied.

Then out of nowhere, a flying suitcase and trunk came for a landing at their feet. Pumpkin glanced over with Nicky as they could witness Tigger coming with several bags all packed with all of Pumpkin's stuff and his stuff too from inside their houses.

"I never thought I'd see a trunk fly," Pumpkin said as Tigger returned to them.

"Well, you can find a flying trunk anywhere," Tigger informed. "I received it from dimension number 2."

"The Lost Luggage?"

"Yep, that's where I got it. These were sold to me. Trust me. These bags will be handy," Tigger said as he placed them into the Boot-Hoot. "What direction shall we take, Pumpkin?"

Pumpkin found himself staring off into space at the luggage inside the Boot-Hoot. The trunk was indeed beautiful. It reminded him of a childhood storybook he had read as a kitten, "The Flying Trunk."

This couldn't be real. That trunk couldn't possibly fly and hold magic. Yet do I believe my eyes? Did I see those bags fly in? Tigger could be pulling my leg, telling me he purchased them in dimension 2.

Just then, he heard his brother yell, "Pumpkin, come on! Stop staring off into space, and let's get going!"

Pumpkin didn't know what to think about these flying trunks or what to take to help guide them.

"I don't know. Did you grab a map?" Pumpkin questioned.

"Yep, it's right here." Tigger opened his luggage, which held an old map of all the dimensional worlds.

The next stop was the Parrot Library, which was a little ways from them as Pumpkin scanned the map further. His eyes then landed on a second star in the northern direction.

Tigger noticed Pumpkin reading the map and asked again, "So what direction do we head in?"

"North," Pumpkin muttered. "We shall head north toward the second star on the right."

"Then let's get going. I ain't getting any younger," Tigger said as he hopped into the vehicle and took a seat in the passenger seat next to the driving wheel.

Pumpkin then turned to Nicky, who stood there with open arms. He embraced him and said, "Take good care of my home. Watch over it, and don't answer the door for any strangers outside of our community."

"Don't worry about it. Your home is safe with me. No invaders shall pass." Nicky winked, giving Pumpkin a hint that it was all going to be fine. "Good luck finding those crystals."

Pumpkin then walked around the Boot-Hoot toward the driver's door. He hopped into the driver's seat and shut the door while Tigger closed up the windows. The clouds in the sky were gathering, and a small storm might be on the way.

Tigger listened to his big brother, turning on the engine, which made a small rattling sound and then began to puff out black smoke from its rear. It let out a loud meow as the headlights came on, giving them a good view of the road ahead going beyond the horizon.

Pumpkin began to put it in drive, and the Boot-Hoot began rolling away from Gramal City, which they called their home. Following the radar Nicky had installed, they headed north.

Nicky could be seen waving goodbye from the rearview mirror as Pumpkin focused heading down the road. Pumpkin waved goodbye, but their cousin was already heading back. He then heard Tigger clear his throat, bringing his attention back to the start of their expedition.

"I can't believe it," Tigger said. "We're finally off on a whole new adventure. A journey better than any other we've had."

"Tell me about it," Pumpkin replied as he glanced at the setting sun on the horizon. It was almost fading from the clouds, making the sky have a nice shade of sapphire and purple as stars began to twinkle right before their eyes. "You and I are going to make quite a team."

They drove for a couple of hours until they got hungry and tired. They managed to find a place to crash for the night and make camp. They made it to a place called Tortoiseshell Beach.

"Look at where we are, Tigger. Tortoiseshell Beach—a place where we've fished with our folks," Pumpkin pointed out. "This is a good place to find dinner and crash for the evening."

"Most excellent. I could use a good, tasty slab of smoked fish." Tigger licked his chops as the thought of hunting salmon in the shallow ends of the water came to his mind. "And especially if you spice it up a little with paprika, dill, and lemon butter."

"Let's get out the fishing rods," Pumpkin instructed. "Do you know where they are?"

"I do. They're packed in the trunk," Tigger said. He went over to the marked trunk that said Fishing Supplies and took out a black rod, which was obviously long enough to be Pumpkin's. His fishing rod was much shorter and lighter.

They even got out a can of worms. Then they sat upon the dock, allowing the salty sea air to give off a cleansing smell of the ocean as they waited for a bite on their rods.

Tigger began to think. "How are we going to find our way to the crystals, Pumpkin?"

Pumpkin didn't answer.

Tigger tried to ask again. "Pumpkin…"

"Huh? What?"

"Did you hear my question?"

"No. Please ask me again."

"Uh…how are we going to find our way to the crystals?" Tigger asked, rather irritated at having to ask him a second time.

Pumpkin said, "I don't know." He was too busy keeping his eye on the fishing line and staring off into the sky. Just then, a streak of light flashed across the sky. *Could that have been a shooting star?* He rubbed his eyes and murmured, "What the? Did you see that?"

"See what?" Tigger could see Pumpkin pointing up at the sky. It didn't take long for another streak of light to come toward them, bewildering him about what he and his brother were viewing.

"I-I can't believe my eyes," Tigger stammered.

"What is that, Tigger? What is that sparkly thing heading right down toward us?"

"I don't know. However, let's hope it comes close enough to check it out," Tigger said, wringing his pawseagerly with anticipation.

Tigger and Pumpkin stood up just as the sparkly round object managed to come flying over their heads toward the green-marsh landmass behind them. *Kerplunk!* A crashing sound echoed throughout the shore.

"Whoever gets to it first is a stinky litter box," Tigger announced, tapping Pumpkin on the shoulder and starting a race toward whatever fell from the sky.

"Hey, no fair! I wasn't ready," Pumpkin said as he raced after his brother.

Pumpkin and Tigger ran around the green marshes only to come to a surprise. What had crash-landed on Tortoiseshell Beach wasn't a rare rock, such as a meteorite from space or any other intergalactic object. What lay before them was a child who was unconscious from her landing.

"A girl!" Tigger shouted. "Pumpkin, there's a girl lying here in the marsh."

Pumpkin bumped into Tigger after he suddenly stopped running, and he too saw the child. There was a girl lying unconscious, and she was covered in mud from the marsh she had landed in.

"What happened to her? I wonder where she's from? Could this be the result of what the mousers were talking about?" Pumpkin asked.

"I suppose it could. I don't really know. Look at her outfit. It has very odd symbols upon it," Tigger pointed out.

Pumpkin noticed what Tigger was speaking about. The girl had long brown hair down to her shoulders, and she was very skinny. She wore a black T-shirt and overalls that had a Japanese message written across her chest.

"Should we leave her here?"

"I don't think so. We should help her."

"Good idea," Tigger agreed. "Let's bring her inside the Boot-Hoot, but be careful moving her."

"Don't worry. I'll be careful," Pumpkin said, understanding Tigger's caution.

They picked up the girl gently. Pumpkin supported her neck as they took her straight into the Boot-Hoot. Inside, they placed her on a small bed in the back and cleaned her up by changing her clothes, making her warm and comfortable. There she remained asleep for the rest of the night as Pumpkin and Tigger took turns watching over her.

While the girl was resting, they went back to check on their fishing lines, and they had dinner ready to be cooked. Pumpkin had caught a giant salmon on his line.

"We can now make those salmon muffins," Pumpkin said as he and Tigger returned to the Boot-Hoot.

"Yeah, salmon muffins. Delicious." Tigger's mind wasn't even on food at the moment. He was too interested in wondering about the girl who had fallen from the sky.

"What's wrong?" Pumpkin asked.

"It's the girl. She's on my mind," Tigger said.

"What about her?"

"What do you plan to do with her when she wakes up?"

"Offer her one of our salmon muffins and talk to her. Find out where she's from and where her parents are and maybe ask her how she's able to fly through the sky," Pumpkin said. "I mean, it must be far away because she seems mysterious having to be someone from the sky."

Tigger said, "Well, it's late right now. Let's have dinner, hit the sack, and we'll figure this girl out tomorrow morning when she wakes up."

Chapter 2

The next morning, Pumpkin woke to find Tigger mixing up more of his favorite salmon muffins and making tea. Across from him in the other bed lay the unconscious girl they had found last night. The smell of salmon muffins baking in the Boot-Hoot's oven filled the air. It was so powerful that it was enough to awaken the girl from her deep slumber as she lay on a warm and comfy bed belonging to one of the cats.

Pumpkin sat up and stretched, allowing himself a long yawn, which grabbed Tigger's attention. He was still mixing up some more salmon muffins.

"Good morning, Pumpkin. Did you sleep well?"

"Yes. I slept fine."

"Good. How's the girl?"

"She hasn't awakened yet," Pumpkin said as he and Tigger crowded the room where she slept. "When will she? I have lots of questions to ask."

"Be patient, my brother," Tigger advised. "Good things come to those who wait."

"Did you notice the land around where we found her? It looks as if a tornado had come through." Pumpkin was speaking about the trees outside the window. So many branches were broken, and the fruit had fallen off the trees.

"Only there was no whirlwind," Tigger said. "Just a girl who fell from the sky. Like a comet."

"A girl with so much mystery to her," Pumpkin commented. "And oh my goodness! Look at this key. It's very strange." He raised his brows then gazed at the child. He had observed a very extraordinary key around the sleeping child's neck. The key itself was made of gold, and it had a rainbow-colored bird at its end.

"I wonder why she wears this key," Pumpkin continued. "It reminds me of the parrot books at Harriet's library we go to all the time. This is our next stop, as I've seen on the map prior to us leaving Gramal City. I'm sure that the key around her neck has a connection to one of the books there. I have just a hunch it does."

"Librarian—you mean Harriett? The parrot?"

"Precisely." Pumpkin nodded.

A groan came from the girl, who then stretched her arms in the air as she yawned.

"Look, she's coming around," Tigger pointed out as Pumpkin watched the girl gain consciousness. She sat up and opened her beautiful brown eyes. She then ran her hands through her long hair, which dropped to her shoulders. She heard Tigger say, "Hello. It's great to have you with us and back with the living."

The girl began to choke out as she sat up and looked around the Boot-Hoot, curiously pointing toward Pumpkin and Tigger, who looked at each other, confused. "Where the heck am I? This isn't the castle. Nor are you the two the guards." She pointed to Pumpkin and Tigger, who looked at each other, still confused.

Guards? They both raised their brows.

The girl stepped out of bed and ran to the window. She could see an enormous sign: "Welcome to Tortoiseshell Beach." She then said rather anxiously, repeating to herself, "Where the heck am I? I'm not in Tortoiseshell Beach, am I?"

"There's no need to have anxiety. You are at one of the most peaceful parts of our realm," Pumpkin explained, making the girl turn to him and Tigger.

"Realm?"

Pumpkin nodded. "Yes. We welcome you to our Realm of Gramal."

"Gramal. That's an unusual name for a kingdom," the girl said with a smile that grew on her face.

She heard Tigger chuckle as he said, "Well, our realm isn't a kingdom. It's really more of a city, where me and my brother reside."

"Oh, my head hurts. And how did I get here, and why am I here with you two?" asked the girl.

"Well, there's the strays, back in our hometown, who are in for a surprise," Tigger mumbled to himself. He then answered the girl, "I can't believe it. You're alive, my dear. Why don't you tell me and Pumpkin who you are and where you're from."

The girl blinked twice as a smile grew on her face. "I am glad I made it here alive, and I am thankful for your hospitality. If you must know, I am from a kingdom from the upper Imaginal Realms. My name is Lauren Kendo. I am a princess."

Pumpkin cocked his eyebrow at her giving herself the title of princess. Really? He didn't know what to say or do except stick a paw out and shake it with her. It was the only way for him to show friendly greetings. He couldn't help gazing at that little bag of hers, wondering what lay inside.

"So, eh…what's in the bag? We're glad to have you here in my little travel home, Your Highness," Pumpkin said.

"Nothing except my little treasures," Lauren said.

"May I see these treasures?"

"Yes, but keep it secret."

"I pinky-swear to it," Pumpkin confirmed as Lauren's eyes teared up. He then asked as he noticed her whipping the teeny water particles away, "What's with the waterworks? I know we've just met, but I am curious."

"I haven't made pinky swears with someone in forever," Lauren told Pumpkin.

"Really. Did something happen?"

"I can't really remember everything because I traveled through the veil of forgetfulness to get here. But I did put a bubble around myself prior to escaping my kingdom so that when I arrive, I would remember most of it," Lauren said as she wiped a tear away. "Sorry if I have a little brain fog. Some of my memory has been erased from traveling through the veil of forgetfulness."

"It's fine. It'll come back to you," Pumpkin said. "Why not show us those treasures? Maybe they'll give your short-term memory a jumpstart, such as that key." He pointed to the colorful charm hanging around Lauren's neck. "Why don't you start with that? Where did you get it?"

"An enormous featherball who runs a library gave it to me," Lauren said as she was trying to fix her brown hair. "Is that what the enormous featherball's name is? I have a book I borrowed from her that I must return. She's pretty crazy for an overly large bird, and with incredibly colorful feathers. I hope her feathers aren't too ruffled because the book I borrowed is overdue."

Pumpkin shook his head. He did not seem really thrilled about Lauren calling the enormous bird (who was completely sane) a featherball. He sighed, closing his eyes and then correcting Lauren on the parrot's name. "Her name is Harriet, Lauren," Pumpkin said with huffiness within his breath. "And that's the librarian's name, and she's not crazy."

"Harriet, you say, has sanity." Lauren's eyebrows raised. "You have to be kidding. I thought she was insane because her name is the same as my crazy aunt's."

What Lauren knew about Harriett the parrot was she was an extremely beautiful librarian with bright colorful feathers covering her enormous body. She was the only big bird Pumpkin knew who could read, and she was not too far from where they were camping.

Pumpkin sighed and said, "We're getting off the subject being discussed."

"Oh. Sorry, Pumpy," Lauren said.

"Don't call me Pumpy, just Pumpkin," Pumpkin grumbled as he returned to the topic at hand. "So why don't we get back on track and settle things with a few muffins?"

Lauren nodded and got up from where she lay. She began to head right for the door. She turned to face Pumpkin with her eyes sparkling and said with a smile, "Do you mind if we use a table outside? I'd rather not take my treasures out inside this contraption of yours. You never know when there's going to be another disaster."

"Not at all," Pumpkin answered. "There's a picnic table out there."

"Excellent," Lauren said as she made her way out the door with Pumpkin and Tigger standing behind her. They glanced at each other before heading out to join her at the picnic table.

Lauren had unfastened the top of her small satchel, turning it over as Pumpkin and Tigger strolled over, anxiously waiting to see and hear about the contents of her bag. She began removing a journal, some spiritual stones, and a flute with some ornate patterns on it. It seemed as if it were signed to do birdcalls, but when you looked at its end, there was a griffin with special engravings of different weather patterns.

"What's this?" Pumpkin picked up the unique instrument. "I've never seen something as rare as a griffin flute."

"Please don't touch that," Lauren barked, grabbing the flute out of Pumpkin's paw, almost pinching him.

"First of all, ouch. And second, why not?" Pumpkin crinkled his eyebrows.

"I don't want claw marks all over it," Lauren said. "That flute is special to me. The griffin I am close with gave it to me."

Lauren then placed the flute back inside the satchel and turned to her journal. The journal was interesting. It had a hard indigo cover with the word *inspire* written in glimmering gold ink. There were even a couple illustrations of moon phases in each corner of the cover. And as Pumpkin watched, Lauren opened the book to reveal its pages, many of which were filled.

Pumpkin couldn't help smiling at her. Most of the pages were specially decorated with gel-pen ink in various bright to warm colors and had a couple of leaves and acorns. But as Pumpkin watched, Lauren came to the last page, and there was a new piece of artwork she had drawn. Lauren had not written on this page because there were no lines. Instead, she used that page to draw a picture of the griffin flute that had been given to her. She was wearing white clothes with a purple belt around her waist in the image she had drawn.

Pumpkin pointed to the drawing. "Is that you?"

"Yep, that's me along with my sensei. The last time I've seen him inside my kingdom doing a lesson at our dojo," Lauren explained as she closed her journal. "I just earned my purple belt."

"What are these crystals?" Pumpkin pointed to five crystals, which were lying on the table next to the flute.

"Oh, those are crystals from the day of my birth," Lauren said. "They were given to me when I was born under the emerald moon—a celebration of Taurus's rebirth. It was a special banquet my mother planned and…" She paused and sniffed the air. "What is that smell?"

"What smell?"

"Don't you smell it?"

Tigger then sniffed the air, becoming aware of the stench. And with his two green eyes, he gazed through the window of the Boot-Hoot. There was smoke coming through. "Hey, Pumpkin."

"What, Tigger?"

"Smoke is coming out the window."

"Huh? Oh no! Please hold your thoughts on those birthstones of yours, Lauren. I had forgotten our salmon muffins in the oven." Pumpkin quickly got up from where he sat. Rushing to unlock the Boot-Hoot door, he ran inside to retrieve the muffins.

Looking through the window from her seat at the table, Lauren watched Pumpkin turn off the oven. Not everyone is perfect when it comes to leaving stuff for too long inside an oven.

"I'm going to see if he needs any help," Tigger said as he too got up from his seat.

Lauren watched Tigger run into the Boot-Hoot to help inside the kitchen, and she rolled her eyes from the interruption.

Pumpkin came out with a tray filled with burnt muffins. He walked to their new guest, placing them on the picnic table.

"I apologize for the interruption," Pumpkin said. "I don't mean to be rude with having the rest of the leftovers from dinner warming up in the oven. Tigger and I were in the middle of making salmon muffins before we had found you and you'd awakened."

Lauren sighed. "It's fine. Besides, I am famished."

"Would you like one?"

"That'll be nice." Lauren nodded. "I am hungry. I don't recall the last time I ate."

"Well, help yourself." Pumpkin held the tray out to her, allowing her to grab one of the fish rolls. "Let me know what you think. It's our first time making them."

Lauren, who was open-minded enough to try a new muffin, had bitten into it. She allowed the sweet-and-sour taste to hit her taste buds along with a hint of smoky paprika. She then looked at Pumpkin standing there, a smile forming as she consumed her share in front of him.

"Well, what do you think?" Pumpkin asked.

"Pretty good, Pumpkin," Lauren murmured as she felt the hunger fade. She felt as if she could cough the muffin she just ate back up. However, she chose to hold back from the idea.

"I'm glad you like them," Pumpkin said with relief as he watched Tigger pass him and sit back down in his seat next to Lauren, who had a great appetite striking her intensely.

A howl echoed from the wind blowing through the forest, making Lauren shiver. She rubbed her right arm as goose bumps grew on her skin.

Tigger noticed the princess shivering, and he began to grow concerned. "Are you cold?"

"Yes," Lauren said. "A little bit."

"Let me get you a blanket while you continue giving us an explanation about those crystals of yours," Pumpkin offered as he walked back into the Boot-Hoot. "Please continue telling us about where you're from. And please tell us all about this extraordinary kingdom of yours that exploded."

Lauren held her head, feeling a headache forming from thinking so hard. "I'm sorry. I can't quite remember the rest of the events still. My brain fog is way too severe."

"Why don't I make you some tea to clear that fog?"

"That'll be great, Tigger. I'll have an easier time remembering," Lauren replied.

Tigger got up and went into the Boot-Hoot to make Lauren a cup of their finest tea—it being the cure for lost memory. He took out a Chinese kettle, and placed it on top of the stove heating up. He then went into the cupboard above and found a box of what were called reishi mushroom tea bags.

The perfect thing for a foggy head, Tigger thought as he grabbed one bag and placed it inside a miniature white Chinese teacup. The kettle whistled, alerting him to shut off the burner. He turned it off and cautiously took the teapot over to the Chinese cup he had waiting on the counter. He then tilted it, allowing the water to fill the cup, letting it create its magic tea.

He came out of the Boot-Hoot. He turned to Lauren with a smile, his eyes beaming as he held the tea out to her. "Here is a cup of reishi tea. And be careful. It's hot."

Lauren took a sip of the tea, and as she did, to her amazement, she began to recall a few things. The few things were the event that came to pass, the break-in of her kingdom, and the return of a mad poet who went by the name Dante. She murmured it under her breath, making the two cats in front of her raise their brows.

"Dante?" Pumpkin repeated. "Who is Dante?"

"Dante is a man who broke into the castle and stole the book with the six crystals that are missing from my bag," explained Lauren. "I was to protect them, but it's unfortunate the other six remain in the book in his possession. This is why I have traveled here—to get the crystals and restore my kingdom. It's why I must go to the library. It may have connections to finding him. Maybe even a portal to the dimension that I am searching to travel. You must help me find Harriet."

Pumpkin let it go, not wanting to push her into telling him things she was uncomfortable with.

"Well, you won't have to look too hard," Pumpkin said as he winked at Tigger, giving off a signal for him to go back into the Boot-Hoot and bring out the map.

Tigger got up again and went into the Boot-Hoot. He came back to the table and placed the map down, rolling it out. There was a huge overview of the documentation building.

Lauren could get a clear overview of the Parrot Library. Her eyes began to sparkle as she grinned to herself while taking a closer look at the parrot statues outside the documentations building, which were holographically moving and making squawking sounds. She could see, underneath the parrot statues, a little twinkling red dot blinking once and then twice. She took her index finger and pushed on it, allowing her print to be scanned.

A generated voice then said, "Parrot Library. In two miles, turn right onto Macaw Lane."

"Gee, you're right. I wouldn't have to go far, Mr. Grumpkins," Lauren agreed with Pumpkin. "Can you please take me there now?"

"Hop in," Tigger said as he rushed to the Boot-Hoot's door, only to trip because Pumpkin had stuck his foot out, making him fall flat on his face.

"Not so fast, bro," Pumpkin said as Tigger picked himself up and dusted off the dirt. "You need to assist with clearing the table first." He pointed to the tray of muffins and other things left upon it.

"Aw, come on, old man. That'll take forever." Tigger growled. "Can't we just leave the table a mess?"

"Nope. It'll be disrespecting the beach," replied Pumpkin. "And besides, if we work together, the work will be finished quickly." He then gawked at Lauren with his green eyes beaming. "And as for you, don't call me Grumpkins."

Lauren shrugged as she gave in, muttering, "Fine." She then glanced around the camping area. "Allow me to give you both a hand with the dishes as an act of gratitude for your kindness."

"We appreciate it." Pumpkin smirked.

Pumpkin then walked to the front (where the front wheel was) and had a seat as he watched from his rearview mirror. Lauren was gathering up the dishes and coming into the Boot-Hoot. She glanced around and then said, "Where do you want the dishes?"

"Place them in the fish sink, right next to you," Pumpkin said, not even looking over his shoulder. He kept his watch on his rearview mirror as Lauren walked up to the fish-shaped sink right next to her and put them down.

Tigger, however, had taken the chair next to Pumpkin and strapped himself in with a safety belt. Lauren didn't know where her seat was going to be. She then cleared her throat, grabbing Tigger's attention. He noticed she was still standing around.

He tapped on his brother's shoulder. "Pumpkin, I know you said no more questions. But what about Lauren? She has no place to sit."

Pumpkin rolled his eyes as he began tapping his clawswith frustration. He then said, after noticing his brother's rudeness, "Of course she has no place to sit. She isn't sitting where I want her to be. However, you are!"

Tigger realized Pumpkin really wanted Lauren to take control of navigation rather than him. He just shrugged his shoulders and got up. He turned to the princess, his eyes beaming at her, "You might as well join him, Princess Lauren. The passenger seat is all yours."

"Why, thank you, Mr. Tigger," Lauren said rather softly as admiration came sparkling inside her brown eyes. "I have a perfect nickname for you, living stuffed animal."

Tigger pressed his lips together and felt his cheeks going all crimson.

"Take your seat, Lauren," Pumpkin instructed. He was sitting behind the driver's wheel. He then placed his key into the slot to start up the engine.

They would head straight for Macaw Lane, where the legendary Parrot Library awaited all newcomers. This was a journey filled with opportunity.

Chapter 3

The entrance to the Parrot Library was still and quiet when Pumpkin, Tigger, and Lauren arrived. However, their arrival was strange and confusing to the two cats. If this was a jungle, then how come there was snow all over the ground? This must be another one of the effects of the crystals, confusing environmental effects where temperatures and the weather got all mixed up. They would find out what happened here and fix it eventually. Right now, they only had to keep an eye on Lauren as she approached the two parrot statues on the left and right side of the library's archway.

The statues were more enormous than the ones on the map as Lauren could observe. In between the statues were the double doors she had an excellent gaze upon. The doors had engravings close to the symbols of her overalls. She continued to stay still as she took in the drawings, which gave a message from years ago. It gave her a tingling feeling inside her tummy.

"According to the map, the graphics upon the entrance may have an affirmation to decode," Lauren declared from her judgment on her analysis.

"Well, why don't you try and decode the affirmation?" Pumpkin pointed out. "Can you try and do that?"

"I could," Lauren said, spotting the hieroglyphics on the two double doors in front of her. She found herself falling to the ground with a thud after getting rather dizzy from thinking too hard.

Tigger rushed up to Lauren. "Are you okay?"

"Yeah. I'm fine, Tigger. I just lost balance while in deep thought," Lauren said, dusting herself off from the frost that lay on the ground.

"Well, maybe when you ponder, you shouldn't do it as deep," Tigger said with caution. "You'll get yourself hurt."

"Yeah, yeah," Lauren said as she began to go back to the brain-work she was doing. Her mind went back to when she tripped. "Tigger, I need you to whip away the frost from the spot I tripped over."

"With my bare paws?" Tigger asked sarcastically. The snow was going to be cold on his pads. It might be so cold, it could hurt because he had no mittens to put over them, and there was a great risk for kitten-bite.

"Never mind, Tigger. I'll do it," Pumpkin said.

"Well, thank you for volunteering, Pumpkin."

Pumpkin then walked up to the spot where Lauren's handprints and bum were marked in the frost. He could see underneath the snow. As he peered closer, a small piece of papyrus appeared. He wiped the snow away to reveal a scroll. "Hey, there's a scroll here. We can use it to decode the message on the door and your clothes, girl."

"Really? Why don't you hand it over," Lauren instructed.

Pumpkin handed the parchment over, allowing Lauren to take a look. He had been correct.

"You are right, Pumpkin," Lauren said as she approached the two double doors again. "There is a message here."

Her eyes focused on the symbols again. She approached the hieroglyphs a little more closely this time, holding the scroll in front of her. And she began to trace the hieroglyphs gently with her fingertips. She drew her fingers back when she finished. She then wiped them on her right cheek, dirtying it up with the scum that covered almost the whole wall.

"What's it say?"

"It says a library left behind waits for a princess who is fair and kind..." Her voice almost trailed off, but Pumpkin gave her an encouraging shove.

"Come on!" Pumpkin said. "Keep reading it."

Lauren began to take a step back and cleared her throat. With a strong, mellow voice, she continued reading the message, "The library left behind waits for a princess who is fair, kind, and strong. She has been unbreakable all along. This year, she will return to find out how strong she is. *Do not* mess with a princess like this."

They waited a few minutes in silence. Suddenly, a rumbling noise came along with a gold light glowing from behind the double doors.

"This library really does belong to her," Tigger said happily, only to get hushed by Pumpkin, who put his finger up to his lips.

Tigger continued to watch with him as the double doors began to rattle and unlock. The parrot statues' eyes (which were diamonds) had blinked twice as their beaks opened. They began to make a squawking sound as the glow behind the door revealed a lit-up and narrow pathway leading into a chamber filled with dusty old shelves covered with vines. And there was warm air, which felt similar to the breath of a monster. It left behind a musty smell—the kind of odor you would get from water that leaks from a cavern.

Tigger's nose did a little tingle at the stench. The stench made him sneeze.

"Bless you," Pumpkin said. "Do you need a tissue?"

"Yes please. And thank you," Tigger said as he felt himself getting ready to sneeze again.

Pumpkin picked out a handkerchief he had inside his back pocket and quickly handed it to him so he could cover his nose.

"Come on. Let's go inside," Lauren said to Pumpkin and Tigger before running on ahead.

Lauren glanced around the room as she and the two cats strolled through. There really wasn't much to witness around the area they were standing in.

She and the two cats could see rows and rows of old dusty bookshelves. She then came to a halt. Ahead of her were three paint-stained windows that had the sun shining its light right through.

The paint-stained windows brought back many memories. The recollections she recalled were the ones she had at church. One paint-stained window showed the one she worshiped the most, Jesus, while the other windows had paintings of her mother holding her as a child.

However, these windows were much more different from the church she had been attending. The last of the paint-stained windows had a picture of her with two traveling cats who had come to the library in search of a book to match a key to some other world.

This must be some part of a prophecy puzzle, Lauren thought as she looked around for Pumpkin. She spotted him at the front desk, where a little sign said Librarian. There was a little bell by a book. It was also a golden parrot, similar to the one on the key she wore around her neck. However, it was much bigger, and it wasn't colorful and old at all.

Pumpkin began to ring the bell, which made a *ding-ding* dinging sound, as if he were going to sign them into a hotel for a temporary stay. He continued to ring the bell. Lauren approached the table to join him, and they waited for a response.

It didn't take long for the sound of beating wings to come as a rainbow parrot with long feminine eyelashes appeared. She was pretty huge and wore small round-framed glasses resting upon her black beak. Her eyes were a deep violet, which sparkled at them as she said with a cheerful smirk, "Tigger and Pumpkin, welcome back!"

"Hidy ho, Harriet," Pumpkin said, his eyes glimmering with warmth. "We've come to return the book we've borrowed."

Tigger brought out a book he and Pumpkin had been reading a while ago. It was an adventure book that had wings upon it too.

"I'm glad you liked it. Are you seeking anything else?" Harriett took it from them. As she touched it with the tips of her wings, the book the cats had read in the last month began to awaken and display behaviors that were out of the ordinary. It began to fly off, heading up the swirling staircase leading to a study room above them.

"As a matter of fact, yes." Pumpkin nodded. "Please step forward, Lauren."

Lauren stepped forward and presented the key she had in between her fingers. "Hi, this key I have was given to me by some bird a while ago. I don't know what it is, but I believe it goes to one of those books you have on those shelves."

Harriett closely observed the key Lauren held in her hand. It then came to her. "Oh yes. I know the book this key belongs to. Come with me. It's inside the Wandering Child section."

Harriett led Lauren toward a stone shelf covered with cobwebs. Lauren thought she could hear a faint hissing sound coming from one of the books. The one making that strange noise was the book Harriett was pointing to. It was the last one on the shelf.

Harriett nodded. "There it is. The book for that key."

"I'll get it," Lauren said. She approached the shelf with the hissing book, which was on the highest shelf, only to find herself unable to grab it. She was way too short. She kept jumping and hopping up and down.

"Here, Lauren. Why don't I get you a ladder so you can climb up and get it," Harriett said as she flew over to the ladder on the other side of the concrete-stone shelf and pushed it toward the girl, bringing it to a halt. "I will stay right here. You go on up and get the book."

Lauren, looking pleased, climbed up to the shelf and grabbed the book while flicking away the spiders and dusting off the cobwebs with her hands. It felt rather sticky, and the dust made her gag and cough. It was hard to breathe from all that dirt. At least, it was now clear enough for her to read the title of the book belonging to her mysterious key.

"*The Light Will Shine the Way*," Lauren read from the cover. She repeated to herself out loud, "*The Light Will Shine the Way?*"

"That's a wonderful name for a story," Tigger said. "Why don't you open it with that key? Maybe it'll take us on some fantastic adventure."

"*No!* Don't open that book!" Pumpkin snapped, grabbing the attention of Lauren and Tigger, who looked at him, rather confused.

"Why not?" Lauren asked, puzzled. "It says *The Light Will Shine the Way*. I am sure it's nothing really horrible."

"That's where you're wrong!" Pumpkin said as he went to grab the book out of Lauren's hands, only to find her moving away from him. "*The Light Will Shine the Way* has nothing good about it. Nothing good can come from it."

"Oh, don't be such a fraidy-cat," Tigger said to his brother. He turned to Lauren. "Go on. Open the book. Show the sourpuss there's nothing to fear."

"You're going to be sorry," Pumpkin warned again. He watched with apprehension as Lauren stuck her key into the keyhole and began turning it in her direction counterclockwise.

The book flicked open, similar to an enchanting old pocket watch from the 1800s. The wind began to pick up from outside the boundaries of the library as the lights began to flicker and then blow out. The library was in eternal darkness, and the princess dropped the book, which remained open on the floorboards. The other books on the shelf began floating eerily around the room, preparing to swirl around the girl and her two comrades.

"What is happening?" Lauren asked.

"I told you. Nothing good comes from it," Pumpkin stated. "You shouldn't have opened the novel."

A bright white light came from the coffee-stained yellow pages surrounding the group as the ghost books swirled around them much more rapidly than usual.

"Hold on tight. Don't be afraid. There is a message here somewhere. Keep calm. It'll be okay. The message will come. Just wait," Harriett instructed.

It didn't take long for the vortex to stop. The glimmering light disappeared as Lauren and her friends opened their eyes. There on the ground was the keyhole book lying at Lauren's feet. It had opened to reveal a map.

Lauren picked up the book to take a look at the map. It was a map of the whole realm she was in. She looked over the pages. She needed to sit down and study this map belonging to the key in order to restore peace to her kingdom again. She sat over in the corner, reading the pages carefully while Pumpkin and Tigger restored order in the library. They were putting the other books that did not have bird features back onto the shelves where they belonged.

Harriett was so happy to have the help. She said with a big grin, "I appreciate your assistance. I don't know what you kids are after here, but it sure was a ruckus."

"It's no trouble." Tigger winked. "But what we're after has big rewards at the end. Wait and see."

"Rewards?" Harriett asked. "What are the rewards Tigger is talking about, Pumpkin?"

"We don't know. However, we are trying to find the book of crystals that got drained of its magic as it had said in this news article we've read in the *Daily Yarn*," Pumpkin explained. "And since we've met Lauren, she has told us some evil guy named Dante, who writes poems, had come along and stolen it directly from her castle, leaving her with five of the crystals while the other six are gone."

"That's terrible!" Harriett said, feeling sympathy for the kingdom that lost its special uniqueness due to the magic being drained. "I hope you guys end up finding the book."

"We will," Pumpkin said, nodding. "Thanks to your willingness to help us find the map from that keyhole book. I'm sorry I made such a judgment about it. I feared we were going to get swallowed by an anaconda."

Harriett made a funny face at the weirdest and creepiest thing Pumpkin had ever told her. There was no way they could be swallowed by a huge snake. She then began to wonder, *Is this what he believed* The Light Would Shine the Way *is about?* She decided to ask him. "Is that what you were fearing as we opened the book?"

"Yes. I've read a book similar to it. It's about a little boy who goes exploring inside the woods behind his house with his very own flashlight," Pumpkin began to explain. "And then he unfortunately winds up being swallowed by a huge snake hiding above him inside the trees, posing as a vine. The end."

Tigger could be heard chuckling inside the background of the library as he picked up the books that had fallen from the nearby shelves. He was laughing at his brother for thinking the book Lauren had opened had the capability of letting a huge snake out magically in order to swallow them all. It was a crazy way of thinking and totally ridiculous. That brother of his was a million laughs!

Chapter 4

Lauren was sitting in the corner, reading over the map on where they needed to go next. On the map, there was an imageof a river cutting through a forest and ending at a mine. She could even see a couple of newer creatures peering from behind the rocks and bushes. Those faces were far and had become unfamiliar. She did not recognize anything like them.

There were antlers sticking above their heads, and there were bird wings stretching out. Maybe it was some kind of mammal waiting to be discovered. Maybe when she found that mammal, it could assist her in finding the crystal.

"How's reading the keyhole book, Lauren?" Tigger asked.

"You should see this, Tigger," Lauren urged with excitement as she got up from where she sat. She eagerly joined him at a small table where he and Pumpkin were resting after helping Harriett clean up the mess the flying books had made. There was a much larger globe of the earth presently upon the table. "As I can analytically observe this strange river, I saw some unfamiliar faces belonging to some unknown creatures. I believe they call this river Bad-Mouther's Brook, home of unknown gossiping creatures."

"Bad-Mouther's Brook!" Tigger said as his brows raised. "Is that the message?"

"Yes. It says we have to go there to obtain the first crystal. The crystal of wisdom."

"That doesn't make any sense." Pumpkin growled as he crossed his arms. "Since when is bad-mouthing filled with wisdom? You would think a crystal would've been placed in a more peaceful environment. Not someplace where there is toxicity to go around. I don't know about this map. It seems rather twisted and funky with its information."

"Look, you wanted to come to this library, didn't you?" Lauren pointed out.

"Yes, I did," Pumpkin admitted, feeling his claws become sharp. He felt as if he wanted to go back in time and hit the reset button. He wanted to have the whole evidence of him hearing about the reward of collecting those crystals erased from his mind. Why, oh why, did he listen to the mousers at that bar he and his brother loved to hang out at so much? He had to listen to them and hear how he could become rich enough to afford the giant pile of bills on his desk. Lauren was right. This whole trip was his fault. He had agreed to help her on this adventure.

Pumpkin could hear Lauren say, interrupting his guilty conscience, "And you said you want to help me find the book so we can put my kingdom back together."

"I did say that," Pumpkin grumbled, making his eyes move back and forth toward his feet. He then gazed back at her, trying not to lose his temper along with the shame he felt, and he did well hiding it. "But I still don't understand. Why Bad-Mouther's Brook?"

"Bad-Mouther's Brook isn't as bad as it seems." Lauren smiled. "Keep an open mind. Trust the map we found. It's much better than that paper one you have that brought us here. And if you ask me, Bad-Mouther's Brook sounds like it would be a gorgeous place to live."

Pumpkin almost struck himself in the face. Lauren had to be kidding.

It didn't take long for Tigger to call out, "Bad-Mouther's Brook isn't a gorgeous place to live, Lauren. How do you know when you haven't visited the area yet?"

"I just do. I have a feeling we're going to run into some fantastic friend or something," Lauren said, her brown eyes as bright as the sun and her smile showing almost angelic. "So let's get going to Bad-Mouther's Brook. You care to join us, Harriett?"

"I am afraid I cannot go," Harriett said with disappointment as she had to reject the invitation the princess had given her. "I have my library to care for, and there are other things for me to do. But I can give you help around here in the library. I suggest you research Bad-Mouther's Brook before visiting. The best of luck to all of you."

Harriett then ascended to the second floor of the library. She failed to notice one of her tail feathers coming loose during her glide. Lauren, however, who had very sharp eyes, rushed to grab it. And she said, "This will make an excellent addition to my natural treasures."

The feather sparkled and shined, much like the key belonging to the keyhole book. It made her very curious.

"What are you doing with the feather?" Pumpkin asked.

"I'm going to add it to my collection and try to see if this feather has magic abilities. It may make it easier for us to find a book on Bad-Mouther's Brook," Lauren said. "There were a couple of books here—besides the keyhole one—that were dusty. They floated everywhere like magic. So I figured if the key is magical, maybe Harriett's feathers are full of magic as well."

Pumpkin chuckled. "Lauren, feathers aren't magic."

"Well, let me prove it wrong," Lauren said. She found another book that was next to the keyhole one they discovered on the same shelf. She then held the feather to its hard brown leather cover. She waited a few minutes. It didn't do anything. "Darn it," she mumbled with defeat. The feather wasn't magic like the key. As Pumpkin had told her, it was completely ordinary.

Lauren could hear Pumpkin giggling at her curiosity on Harriett possibly having magical abilities in her feathers. Unlikely. He then said, "You are too much." He walked right past her over to a barrel where a bunch of scrolls with writing lay.

The barrel had a sign over it. It read, "Scrolls from the Ancestors. Choose one wisely." There were lots of things written upon them, and they were really special because the ancestors that wrote upon them had passed to some other world and had to leave their work behind.

Pumpkin closed his eyes, taking his time. He moved his hand over them a few times, and then he found the right scroll. He chose wisely. He found one that had much information from a spirit who was known to be a protector of its people at Bad-Mouther's Brook.

"Bad-Mouther's Brook has a white wolf spirit that looks after them," Pumpkin said after he finished reading the scroll. "It sounds as if this town we're going to be visiting next is cursed."

"A white wolf spirit looking after a cursed town?" Lauren repeated, cocking an eyebrow. "Really? I never heard of a white wolf spirit. Let me read that story in the scroll."

Pumpkin gladly handed the scroll over to Lauren. Lauren began to read it herself. The scroll had a legendary story that told the tale of a young boy who was right around her age. He had dark brown hair, dark green eyes, and had a frail and stalky build to him. He was on the run for his life after he had witnessed some horrors going on inside the town. A fire had broken out and destroyed his home. His mother, father, and brother told him to run for it. Do not look back. He glanced behind him anyway and saw a monkey warrior swinging its weapon and letting out a vicious mutant hoot-call to its pack. They joined him in a war cry to signal they would hunt the boy down.

But why would these mutant animals want to harm an innocent boy with a heart filled with pure fire that would never blow out no matter how many times one dared to bring him to the underworld? These apes must be really demonic, blackhearted, and vain creatures to do such horrible acts. A painful scream then ripped out through the forest as he ran, making the black birds scatter among the trees where he took a dive behind to hide within the shadows.

The boy was trying to see if he could fool his enemy and avoid the sharp spears that were being thrown at him. The scream came again, sounding much closer to where he stood, and it was familiar to him. His green eyes grew wide.

"Mother!" he screamed as it faded and more hooting sounds took over with triumph. "No!" He could sense his eyes become glossy with tears as he then had to continue going in the direction he was heading at a quicker pace. As he came into a clearing, he had to slow down from jogging really hard. He stopped before reaching the cliff edge, where a waterfall was running. He could see the raging water running rapidly. He thought to himself, *I'm scared to jump. The rapids are going pretty fast. However, I have to because if I don't, the apes that murdered my mother will slaughter me.*

Another violent roar shook throughout the enchanted forest. The boy turned around and noticed a much larger ape coming to stand near him upon a sharp boulder. He looked at it, his fearful green eyes connecting with the ape's larger ruby eyes. The filthy ape had sweat dripping down his back, as the teeny furs on his neck stood up, and his red eyes beamed with excitement.

They were now ready to go in for the kill. The killing of a young boy was on this huge ape's mind in a heartbeat. He had been waiting to do this for a very long time. The enormous ape hooted again, giving off orders that only the boy could understand. Appearing from behind the bushes were groups of mutant apes of all sizes. They began to surround him. The boy had read the larger ape's eyes and mind pretty clearly. It said, "Kill him."

The boy began backing up, and he bumps into another ape behind him. They got into a huge scuffle. He did fight with all his might to try and save himself.

However, he found himself unable to. He could see one ape with a dagger now pressed up against his chin as it sat there on his chest, ready to cut him up as they had him pinned to the ground. This was just as the boy feared. This was the end of the road for him. Just as everything looked its darkest, an interruption came in the form of a mysterious howl. They could hear the sound of an animal running on all fours as it came through the forest.

The group of apes paused and looked in the direction it was coming from. There was nothing except a glow of white light and the forest mist coming to surround the boy and the apes. The boy thought that it was strange. In the woodlands, this had never happened before. When it subsided, the apes shook it off and decided to resume what they were doing. The beast was about to proceed with slitting the boy's throat, but as the boy closed his eyes, something suddenly lunged at the ape, pushing it off and away from him. The ape that held the dagger had been knocked into his followers, who were about sixteen feet away from him.

The young boy opened his eyes. He found himself witnessing a wolf, as white as the arctic, standing there in front of him. She turned her head to look at him from the corner of her silver eyes as she let out a violent growl, scaring the apes.

The apes dropped their weapons and ran as hard as they could, leaving the boy standing there with the minor cuts he had received. He was feeling quite tired. He found everything now going dark, and he collapsed to the ground with his body aching all over. He lay there, letting the darkness take over his mind as the vision of the enchanted forest and the white wolf faded. This concluded the story.

"That's it?" Lauren questioned as she didn't see anything more on the story. "The ending of the tale leaves me hanging with questions. Is this boy still alive? What is the wolf's name? Do you know anything about this wolf, Pumpkin?"

"Yes. I do know a little about it. The apes were an issue back in the day, some time before your kingdom exploded," Pumpkin informed her. "However, there aren't many of them left. I believe most have failed or passed on due to us cats taking over, enslaving them and then having them banned. Their deadly remains are probably somewhere in the desert as a forever grave. That's where we've placed them during the rest of their entire lives."

"Okay. Besides that, how long have they been residing in the desert?"

Pumpkin couldn't believe Lauren was being compassionate toward the apes. It was a little bit disturbing to see that. You would've thought she'd hate that they tried to kill an innocent little boy. He then said, "Geez, you're really loving."

"I'm always loving. If those apes have attacked this boy, then there must be a reason for it," Lauren said. "He must be guilty of something. I scorn the wolf for saving him."

"Now, Lauren," Pumpkin warned, "you haven't met the boy. And besides, this was a long time ago as I have said. You weren't even born in that period of time. And besides, things happen for a reason. For whatever reason, the boy had been protected by the wolf spirit."

"Enough about the wolf spirit," Tigger interrupted as the two were discussing the matter. "Are we going or not? It's almost late afternoon."

Pumpkin reached into his pocket and found his pocket watch almost pointing to twelve. His brother was right. They needed to get a move on. "Yeah, let's get going."

Lauren nodded and began to rush ahead of them back to the Boot-Hoot. "I have to check out this town in order to find out more information."

Pumpkin and Tigger looked at each other as they watched Lauren dash through the double doors of the library. They sighed and then ran after her, ready to begin the next part of the adventure. They were off to Bad-Mouther's Brook.

Chapter 5

Bad-Mouther's Brook was home to a man who went by the name Edward Cuddlebuggle, who led his people by working hard at engineering and inventing. He lived in a house that was half-barn and half-windmill. Containing chipped paint walls, it was filled with cobwebs and spiders after it had been signed with spray-paintings of crude remarks. This building was built about sixty-three years ago to stand strong on a high cliff overlooking the entrance to the brook. It would make guests feel like they were greeted with the town's rottenness, for the people who lived there were overly critical and rude to each other.

It was the middle of the night when Pumpkin drove the Boot-Hoot through the town. They were passing the sign as he stated, interrupting Lauren's gaze toward the town, "We're almost there!"

"That's great," Lauren said. She couldn't wait to find out more about this town and where the crystal of wisdom was located. "Which way shall we go?"

Tigger said, pointing toward a three-pointed sign, "There is a sign pointing toward the northeast direction right through here. I suggest we take it because I hear around this part of the forest leading to Bad-Mouther's Brook, the people work hard here at engineering, and inventions are pretty crude. We shouldn't run into them."

"Really?" Lauren's eyebrows raised.

Tigger nodded as he pointed to the sapphire sky above them. "See for yourself. There are wood elves flying above."

Lauren glanced out the window of the Boot-Hoot as Pumpkin continued to drive on through, passing the three-pointed signs.

Lauren then could see the group of flying elves the two cats had just warned her about soaring around and working hard in very big groups. Her jaw dropped as she watched them go on with their evening in their squirrel costumes throughout the region. Passing them as they followed the brook Pumpkin had been traveling along, she witnessed one of the elves come to a run-in with one person who seemed to be an elf. However, as she looked much closer, he didn't look much like an elf but more of a human boy.

"Hey!" She heard the elf growling. "Watch where you're going, Cuddlebug klutz."

"I'm sorry, sir. Excuse me. I didn't mean to bump into you on purpose. I bumped into you by accident, so why don't you watch your judgments of character when you first meet somebody? You could end up getting your melons knocked out," the human boy said with a warning.

The middle-aged elf grabbed the boy by the scruff of his costume. "Now tell me, boy. Have you ever experienced losing your melons, boy? It's painful."

Lauren couldn't believe how the middle-aged elf had talked to the boy after they had bumped into each other by accident up there. She then said to Pumpkin, "Did you hear that? The boy told the middle-aged elf that bumping into him was an accident. And also, the boy had warned him the next time he bumps into anyone else and judges them, it's going to get them in very big trouble. The middle-aged elf may get his melons knocked right in the kisser. But the elf man doesn't care and looks as if he's going to beat the boy up. We should help him."

"What do you expect? People who are polite to others are the ones who get kicked inside their melons here," Pumpkin told Lauren. "As you probably had read very clearly inside the scroll you picked out about Bad-Mouther's Brook back at the Parrot Library."

"Well, maybe I could change the way the elves are talking to each other. I would teach them that they shouldn't knock anyone inside the melons for being polite," Lauren said, making a suggestion. "They do need their manners to bring great respect. Especially toward me, since I am a princess that's going to be passing on—"

"Let's move along," Pumpkin said as he then began to drive on, not wanting to further discuss the town's ugly attitudes. "I want to continue following these signs. It'll probably give us a five-minute shortcut to Bad-Mouther's Brook, never mind the long way of following these signs. Thank God we're underneath a second star."

It didn't take long for a sudden spark from a flame to come from the human boy who was hanging inside the sky, trying to get loose from the middle-aged elf's grip on the scuff of his shirt. He then took notice of his costume, which was burning and smoking, and said, "Hey, what's wrong with my costume?"

The middle-aged elf who was giving him trouble chuckled and said, "Why don't I give you a hand there, pal, with your right jet engine?"

"No, I've got this," the boy said.

"Oh nonsense. I and my father are willing to assist since you had mentioned on knocking out melons." A female fairy came along full of sass as her two eyes (each being a different color) glowed with rage toward the human boy. She obviously had been adopted by these elves and didn't appreciate him being polite to her father. She looked at the engine and said, "Oh, I see what the problem is. Allow me to tighten that screw for you."

"No, wait. It's fine," the boy said, but he could feel the fairy continuing to mess with the jet engine.

"That should do it. Let him loose, Father," the fairy said.

The middle-aged elf let go only to hear a halting of the right engine wing as it began to fall apart. More smoke came, and the left jet-engine part of the boy's flying squirrel costume started to burn and smoke.

"What did you do to my engine?" the boy asked.

"You know how I received your warning from you that your melons would hurt when they're knocked out, boy?" the middle-aged elf said, making the boy panic. "Well, enjoy your fall to experience that kind of pain!" They waved good luck to the boy as he began to plummet down.

Lauren took notice because of her sensitive hearing, and with panic in her eyes, she said, "Pumpkin, come on! We need to help the boy! That no-good fairy had really messed up his jet engine!"

Pumpkin looked away from the road he was following once again and watched as the boy she was begging him to assist came rapidly down toward the Boot-Hoot's windshield. "He's falling down pretty rapidly. I'll push this red button and—"

Before he even could push any buttons, the boy came with a *kersplat!* upon the Boot-Hoot's windshield. It was a meaty thud.

Pumpkin proceeded to push a red button, making the wipers whip the boy off the windshield and causing him to fall to the ground, which was full of mud puddles. He then brought the camper to a halt right in their tracks.

"I'm going to talk to him," Lauren said, getting up from her seat as she rushed to the Boot-Hoot's door. She turned around. "Aren't you both coming with me?"

"I'll go with you," Tigger said, getting up from his seat. "I would like to meet this boy. Maybe he could help us. What about you, Pumpkin?"

"I need to clean the windshield. It's ruined with hand and face prints. I can't travel in these conditions. You two go on ahead."

Lauren shrugged at Pumpkin and then left with Tigger through the door.

The boy had picked himself up and was dusting himself off as they approached. He fixed his glasses and took a glance at what went wrong with his flying-squirrel suit. *Just my luck*, he thought, frustrated. *Both of my jet engines have gone haywire because that fairy ruined it after I said I was sorry for bumping into her father by accident. Man, she has a horrible attitude similar to everyone else here. She's probably not worth a date.*

He then searched for the other broken engine. He found a hair clip inside. *These must be my sister's clips that got stuck inside my engine.* He held up a diamond hair clip, which had a few pearls. He failed to see Lauren coming up from behind him. She cleared her throat, making him jump back and twirl around as he clasped a hand on his heart. "Ah!"

"I'm sorry," Lauren said. "I didn't mean to frighten you."

The boy regained his composure when he saw Lauren, and he crossed his arms. He wrinkled his eyebrows as he said with denial, "Oh, you don't scare me. You're a girl. I ain't scared of sissy girls."

"How rude. I am not a sissy," Lauren pointed out. "I'm far from it because I am a princess. Anyway, that's no way to talk to me. And besides, I am not from this area of Bad-Mouther's Brook, and neither are my two friends. Can you please tell us the directions to finding the crystal of wisdom?"

After Lauren asked her question, she could see that the boy who was dressed in a flying-squirrel costume was barely listening to her.

The boy was too busy fiddling around with his jet engines. He had his mind occupied with wanting to deal with his older sibling when he got home. She was going to be in trouble with their mother. She had been told that she needed to be more mindful of where she kept her hair products. She could hurt someone. He heard Lauren clear her throat, which grabbed his attention again. "Oh, I'm sorry. Did you say something?"

"I said I ain't from this area," Lauren said, repeating herself. "And neither are my friends, who are from Gramal City. We came to your part of town searching for a crystal. I don't suppose you know where it is?"

A crystal? Does anything like that ring a bell to him? He decided to ask about it. "So you're looking for a crystal. Let me guess. Is it blue, gray, and green? Does it radiate peaceful energy?"

"Yes. Have you seen it?"

"Yes, and I cannot help you," the boy said.

"Why not?" Lauren asked.

"It's not my problem," the boy said. "You will have to find it on your own."

Lauren turned to Pumpkin for some guidance as he was finishing up with cleaning the windows and the shield. He shrugged along with Tigger. There was nothing they could do.

"Oh, never mind. We might as well be moving along," Lauren said. She turned to Pumpkin and Tigger, saying, "We better move on. He cannot help us around here."

"Oh well," Pumpkin said. "I was sure we'd be able to find that crystal, especially with your family holding a reward—"

"Did you say reward?" the boy asked as an idea came to his mind. Maybe if he helped them, they'd share it with him after they returned the crystals.

"Yes. Pumpkin did say reward." Lauren nodded. "My family and I are holding it for whoever finds the crystals and returns them to us."

"Well, I change my mind considering there's some reward you're going to get for the return of the crystals," the boy said to Lauren with an extended hand and a smile. "I am sorry for being rude. I didn't mean to address you as a sissy princess."

"I appreciate the apology. What do they call you around here?"

"Call me AJ. However, my name is Andrew Jr."

"Well, it's a pleasure to meet you, Andrew. I am Princess Lauren," Lauren said, accepting the handshake. She noticed how soft his hand felt in hers.

Man, he's sensitive. I like him, Lauren thought to herself.

It didn't take long for something to drop at Andrew's feet. A tool had fallen out of his black jacket pocket. She became curious as she observed Andrew snatching the tool right back up and putting it back inside his pocket. "What was that?" she asked.

"Oh nothing. Just a tool from my workshop at home," Andrew said.

"What kind of tool?"

"I'll explain later. However, you cannot take your traveling device with you." Andrew pointed to the Boot-Hoot sitting there in park mode. "Leave it where it is."

"If we leave it here, where would we sleep for the night?" Pumpkin asked.

"My house," Andrew said with an offer. "You all can stay tonight. My folks wouldn't mind new visitors. Follow me."

Lauren, Pumpkin, and Tigger followed Andrew in the direction of his house.

Along the way, Lauren began drifting off deep into her thoughts, pondering about this boy she just met. She admired his jet-black hair, his green eyes behind his glasses, and his stocky build. If there was one thing she admired most about a guy, it was his eyes. His green eyes reminded her of the ocean and how gentle it was. She feels good about meeting someone around her age. She noticed him stopping on the hill upward, making her come to a halt beside him.

Down below, she couldn't believe her eyes as the sun was setting behind the mountains. Beyond Bad-Mouther's Brook, she could see the buildings of the city below all lit up. She took a good look. There was something gorgeous about seeing the city below all lit up.

"Wow, everything looks wonderful up here," Lauren pointed out. She then noticed vandalism all over the windmill. "Except for that."

Andrew looked at the drawings left behind by the vandals and said, "I know the gangs have done this. I've asked about them around town. Stay away."

"So tell me about your family. What are they like?" Lauren asked.

"My family is welcoming. Although…" Andrew seemed to have a change of mind. "Just as a heads-up, they're not always a typically normal, day-at-the-beach family."

"What do you—"

"*Andrew Jacob*!" shrieked a motherly voice. A woman appeared from their house. She was mighty in her appearance with all that muscle, and she wore her hair up in a ponytail while the rest of her looks were very Western—almost old-fashioned, as if she could wrestle a few hogs to the ground. However, she did have a gentle heart deep down.

"Who's that, Andrew?"

"My mom, Lauren. Her name is Terri," Andrew said as he began trotting down the hill to find out what she wanted from him.

Lauren blinked twice and then followed him with Pumpkin and Tigger trailing behind.

"What is it, Mom?" the boy asked.

"I need you to pick up your room," Terri told Andrew.

"Aw, Mom. Now? I mean, I just met a girl and—"

Andrew was cut off as Lauren came face-to-face with his mother. "Hello, ma'am. I don't suppose you have heard of me, but I am Princess Lauren. I am just cutting through the neighborhood—"

"Get out of town! You're the princess?" Terri said, somewhat shocked.

"Yes, I am. I am from the kingdom that—"

"Blew up? We know. We've heard about you. You are missing all over the news. Are you all right?"

"I'm fine." Lauren nodded. "I am trying to find the rest of the seven crystals."

"Well, I'm sure you'll find them. Now excuse me," Terri said, returning to her son. "I need you to pick up your room, Andrew. Your cousins Gurdy and Brody are coming, and I need you to watch them."

Just at hearing about his younger twin cousins Gurdy and Brody coming to his house and the mention of babysitting made, Andrew's ears stung at the thought of it as a chill ran down his back. His blue eyes were filled with horror. It was even worse when you had just made a new friend. They would probably chase her away too as they had done with his last girlfriend. He then said to his mother, "Please, Mom, not Gurdy and Brody. They can't come here. Today's not a good day."

"I'm sorry, Andrew, but I really need you to pick up your room before they arrive tomorrow," Terri said. She then looked at Lauren. "Why don't you come in, make yourself comfortable for now. It's getting dark."

"Thanks, ma'am," Lauren said. She willingly came into the house with Pumpkin and Tigger following close behind her.

Terri almost closed the door on them. It caused her to stop and face the two cats. She could see they had used their hands to keep her from shutting the door, including their feet. "Who are you guys?"

Lauren turned around and saw the two cats standing there. "Oh, I'm sorry, ma'am. They're with me. Meet Pumpkin and Tigger. They discovered me at Tortoiseshell Beach and are allowing me to hitch a ride with them to search for the crystals."

"We're helping her, ma'am," Pumpkin said.

"Come inside. We would not mind having cats around, especially now due to the investigation of mice scurrying around every corner of our home," Terri told Pumpkin and Tigger.

"Investigation of mice?" Tigger raised his brow as Pumpkin shut the door behind him. "Are you saying the mousers were here? Are they the same ones from Gramal City? The ones Pumpkin met at the bar—those mousers?"

"Yes, they had dropped by to ask for assistance. They wanted to team up with our family and our business," Terri explained. "They know we're very skilled at finding rare and priceless lost jewels. They've asked us to keep our eyes peeled for you, Lauren, and turn you in when we have found you. However, I felt sorrow about that idea of having to turn in a jewel like you. I had decided not to. You seem way too valuable to be turned in to the mousers."

Lauren felt her cheeks grow warm. This was true. She was a priceless and rare gem to find. Surprisingly, she didn't know how Terri seemed to know that without knowing her for more than a few hours. Maybe it was the vibe she gave off with her bright brown eyes and the almost angelic features to her appearance, complete with a heavenly smile.

"Andrew," Terri said, gaining her son's attention, "why don't you show Lauren what you've been working on in your workshop?"

"Um, sure." He grabbed Lauren by the hand and said, "Come along. Wait until you see what I've been doing inside there."

Lauren smirked and said, "Okay." She turned to look Pumpkin and Tigger directly in the eye and asked, "Do you mind if I…?"

"No," Pumpkin said. "Go on. Tigger and I want to speak to Terri about the other lands."

Chapter 6

Andrew and Lauren walked together on the narrow streets of Bad-Mouther's Brook. An awkward silence went on between them for a couple of minutes. To Lauren, this felt very awkward. She then decided to get a conversation started.

"So, Andrew," Lauren began, grabbing his attention, "what can you tell me about that tool I saw earlier?"

"Tool?"

"Yeah. The one that fell out from your pocket."

"Oh, um, it's a chisel I use when I am in the mines. I use it to get jewels I find unstuck from being in very strong rocky walls within the mines. I take them back to my family's workshop afterward to make things out of them." He reached into his pocket and pulled out the chisel she saw.

It was incredibly small and seemed as if it could be about the size of a toy. However, it was a real one with a blade that could cut through either wood, rocks, or stone. Lauren looked at the tool for a couple of minutes. She then said, "Must've taken a lot of skill to use one."

"No, there really is not much experience you need," Andrew said as he adjusted his glasses, which were beginning to fall from his nose. "I was pretty basic when I had started using it for the first time. My stepdad taught me how to use it safely so I don't hurt myself."

A crumbling sound came from behind them, along with a shattering of glass. Andrew and Lauren stopped in their tracks out of curiosity. They turned around, suspecting someone might be following them close behind. There was no one to be seen, just an empty alleyway with a broken bottle of rum that had fallen from a barrel. They looked at each other and shrugged it off.

"Weird," Lauren said, standing her ground as if she were almost ready to meet some complete stranger who was hiding in the shadows. "It was just a bottle of rum smashing to pieces. To my surprise, I sure felt as if someone was stalking us from behind, didn't you?"

"Yeah, it gives me the shivers. However, let's forget about it and continue to the workshop belonging to my stepdad. It's around the corner. This way."

Lauren and Andrew hurried along the brook, leaving whoever was following them behind in the dust. Appearing from around the corner was a boy with short brown hair, fiery blue eyes, and light peach skin holding a flat expression. He watched them leave with hatred growing inside his body toward Andrew, especially if he was with that new girl who held a smile and was happy as always to see everyone. He admired her deeply. He would indeed have to follow them into those mines because he too was hunting the same crystal.

This is going to be a lot of work, the boy thought to himself. *It's better if I allow Andrew and that new weird, strange girl who I have a crush on to do all the work. It makes it easier for me.*

The shop was a little dark through the windows when Lauren and Andrew arrived. However, glowing behind the glass were a few well-designed necklaces, bracelets, and earrings nicely laid out together.

Lauren felt awestruck with the first one that caught the glimmering twinkle inside her right dark-brown eye. The first amulet for her to fall in love with was the key with the white diamonds in the shape of a heart.

Lauren said, "That's pretty and sparkly."

"Yeah. It's one of our projects we're doing," Andrew revealed as he pulled out a key to the shop to unlock the door. "I have more I'm still working on inside."

"I'd love to see them," Lauren said.

"Come on in. And by the way, watch your step." Andrew pointed to the stoop he just stepped upon. "This stoop is a bit tricky. It can make you fall on your face if you are not careful."

Lauren took a giant leap over the stoop, allowing her feet to land on the dusty and creaky old floorboards. Inside the shop, she could see a bunch of crystal figures were on display, each one having a price tag on it. Her eyes landed upon Andrew's work desk. One of them looked similar to a dolphin out in the ocean. She heard him flicking on a light that brightened up the room they were in. He took out from his other pocket the hair clip that got caught in his flying-squirrel costume, which he was still dressed in. He had not yet changed out of it. He took a seat at his desk and placed the hair clip down.

Andrew then switched his glasses with another pair that allowed him to peer closer at his sister's hair clip. There was a crack in one of the pearls. This could easily be fixed. Lauren, who was standing around, was finding herself sidetracked. Instead of the diamond key necklace, she ended up falling in love with the glass dragon standing on display. It was hard not to.

Lauren began to reach out for it when Andrew interrupted her. "Don't touch anything."

"Why not? It's so sparkly inside here, and gorgeous," Lauren said.

"And fragile," Andrew warned her again. "Everything in these displays is breakable."

"I know," Lauren said. "I handle my mother's good china all the time. She trusts me, unlike my aunt who I hate to mention." She began to shake off those thoughts in her head about her aunties driving her nuts.

Andrew, however, was coming to a form of understanding of relatives being on your nerves. "Relatives driving you crazy?"

"Yep. Up the wall," Lauren growled. "They drive me, as always, insane."

"What do they do that is so bad?"

"I'll tell you," Lauren began. "They treat me like a baby, even if I am thirteen."

Andrew knew how it felt to have family members that do extremely embarrassing things. He vowed to keep things he and Lauren discussed in private. He would not tell her relatives anything unless she gave him permission to. However, he could not help laughing a little about it because Lauren was being silly. He then said something to make her lighthearted about it.

"You must be really special to be babied by them," Andrew said.

This made Lauren cock an eyebrow on what he meant. There couldn't be anything special about a princess surviving a catastrophic attack. He had to be kidding. Lauren decided to ask him, keeping her cool. "What do you mean by special? I see nothing extraordinary about me."

"You survived your kingdom exploding, didn't you?" Andrew cocked an eyebrow, copying Lauren's facial expressions and revealing his cocky side. "It takes a strong person to survive an event, making you into a victor."

Just after Andrew spoke the word *victor*, a sudden blast came from behind Lauren, and the store alarm went off.

He got up from his desk and went right over to the front store window, where a hole was found. He could see out the window. There was a boy with brown hair, dressed in dark clothing, making a run for it down the street.

Lauren noticed him too, and she then asked, "Who was that, Andrew?"

Andrew said, very puzzled and feeling slightly nervous and not really wanting to honestly answer her, "I don't know. However, he left this rock behind with a demonic cross painted on it."

Andrew picked up the rock in order to observe the cross further, allowing Lauren to get a good view. There was definitely a demon drawn on it. The creature from the underworld had a long forked tongue. And what's this—snakes for hair? That was strange. She would place her judgment on it. It was good to judge odd symbols left behind with a shattered window.

"I am sorry about your window," Lauren empathized. "I don't know who in their right mind would—"

"Don't be sorry for me. I deserve it. Why don't we go to my house?" Andrew said, cutting Lauren off. "I need to tell Tom. He may not enjoy the news. However, it's best."

Tom was outside, working on his motor vehicle, when Lauren and Andrew returned to the house. He was an enormous man, as large as Lauren imagined her own father to be. He had a small goatee growing on his face. His gray hair was long and tied into a ponytail while his eyes were an ocean-blue filled with joy for treasure and adventures. He did not hear his stepson calling to him as they approached him from behind.

"Thomas! Thomas!" yelled Andrew.

"What is it, kid?"

"Some strange boy threw a rock at our store window," Andrew explained, showing him the demonic rock.

"Are you serious?" Tom asked. He looked at Lauren, and she nodded.

"It's true, sir," Lauren added, talking rather rapidly along with Andrew at the same time. "We were talking about jewelry projects when we heard the window smashed—"

Thomas put his hands up, silencing both of the kids. He then told them, "You two go inside and calm down. No need to get excited. I will discuss this with your mother."

"Don't you believe us?" Andrew asked.

"I do. I just want to involve your mother in this also," Thomas said. "Especially if this rock has a demon on it."

Lauren and Andrew looked at each other at the mention of Terri getting involved with this kind of situation. Usually, you do not want to involve anyone who may be disturbed by a rock that could belong to a Hellion or Satan follower for that matter.

Andrew then felt something under the rock. "Wait a minute. What's this?" He found a note stuck at the rock's bottom. It said, "There's no greater sorrow than to be mindful of the happiest moments in misery."

"Well, that's a little off-kilter," Lauren said after Andrew read the note out loud. "There are no happy times when anyone is miserable."

Pumpkin and Tigger could be heard finishing their conversation with Terri as they walked through the front door. Terri noticed Andrew and Lauren coming into the house after speaking with Pumpkin. Tom gave Andrew an encouraging shove to speak up about it.

"Mom, do you have a minute?"

Terri smiled at her son as he and Lauren stood in front of her. "What is wrong, kiddo?"

"Mom, we found this demon rock by our shop window, which was smashed. Apparently, some odd, very mad boy had thrown it," Andrew said, glancing around as if he was suspecting another attack.

"Did you speak with Tom?"

"He has spoken to me, Terri," Tom said. "I wanted to see what you'd make of all this action that just happened."

Terri pondered a few minutes after hearing about the rock the two kids had discovered. "Let me look at this rock a little closer."

Andrew held out the demonic rock in the palm of his hands. Terri couldn't believe her eyes. Both of the kids may be in danger. She then said, "I need to take this rock straight to the half-barn, half-mill conservatory. I believe Edward Cuddlebuggle would be suspecting things like this to occur."

"Edward Cuddlebuggle? You mean the man of engineering and innovation?" Andrew asked.

"That's him," Terri said.

"Who is Edward Cuddlebuggle?" Lauren asked.

"He's the man of this whole town. He knows everything, especially strange crystals and rocks like this yet to be discovered," Terri explained. "What's also interesting about him is his knowledge about demons, which are attracted to some wisdom crystals."

"Hey!" Lauren declared. "I'm looking for that crystal. Can I go with you to meet Edward Cuddlebuggle?"

Terri and Tom looked at each other and said, "No."

"No? What do you mean no? I need to have that wisdom crystal that belongs to my family," Lauren said.

"I know it does. However..." Terri cleared her throat as she continued, "You never met Edward Cuddlebuggle before, and he's never met you. It would be rude of me to bring some completely strange guest to his home without his permission. And besides, after this disturbing rock has been thrown and destroyed our shop window, I would rather if you both please stay here at our house where it's safe. This has now become a strict business meant for grown-ups."

Lauren crossed her arms and grumbled to herself. Andrew, however, placed his arm around her. He whispered in her ear, "Let it go, Lauren. We might as well stay hidden as my mother is saying.

Besides, it's past my bedtime." He was getting tired and was yawning at the thought of it, and he could see Lauren was as well. She was yawning after him, and it grabbed Pumpkin's attention.

"You two hit the sack," Tom said to the two kids.

"But I'm not even tired," Lauren continued to protest, letting out another little yawn.

"Come on, Lauren," Andrew said. "You are getting too tired."

Andrew then heard Pumpkin say to Terri and Tom, "You and your husband should go to Edward Cuddlebuggle's. Me and Tigger will watch the kids. How does that sound?"

"Perfectly fine," Terri said. "And keep a close eye on Andrew. He can get pretty hyperactive, so make sure he doesn't eat any sugary things before bed such as gum or—"

"Mom, I'm almost thirteen. I don't need anyone to watch me." Andrew growled, his cheeks turning red as he crossed his arms.

Lauren couldn't help chuckle with empathy a little, remembering earlier tonight on their discussion inside the shop about having tolerance toward her aunt's doing this to her. She could see how he did understand her.

"It's not funny."

Lauren stopped and said, "I'm sorry, Andrew." She began to repeat what he said to her. "Don't you think it's wonderful that your mother cares for you?"

"No," Andrew grumbled. "It's overbearing."

"Ooh, somebody's a crankypants," Lauren said.

"All right. Good night, you two." Pumpkin pointed to the staircase leading up to Andrew's sleeping chambers.

Andrew and Lauren headed up the staircase, peering through a small window as they watched Terri leave with Tom. They were heading off to see Edward Cuddlebuggle.

Andrew sighed again. He then said under his breath, "I wish we could've gone." He followed Lauren into his sleeping chambers.

She was already sound asleep on his cushion bed. He climbed in with her, blowing out the candle next to him.

Chapter 7

The home of Edward Cuddlebuggle above the mining grounds had two giant pillars engraved with weather patterns, and it had a large tyrant sticking out of each, holding a flag of importance. This building had been called Bad-Mouther's Point. It was written clearly on one of the flags Terri and Tom had passed by before coming through the double doors right before the waterfall, which held the symbolism of a fox wrestling a weasel. The couple could see this after passing the flags and the waterfall. There was a balcony above their heads belonging to the great man they had come to visit.

Terri picked up a few pebbles from the ground and began to throw them gently toward the double doors to create a *tap-tap-tap* sound where Edward had his curtains drawn closed. She could hear the old man groaning. They got a good view of Edward Cuddlebuggle stretching and yawning above them as he pulled himself out of bed while scratching his rear end. He walked across the bedroom's creaky old floorboards and pulled on the string to move the curtains in front of him to give him a view of his front yard.

"Hello?"

"Terri," Edward said with a little crankiness, "you better have a good reason for waking me up in the middle of the night. Hope it improves my mood."

"It will. Trust me," Terri said as she came before him and proceeded to tell the elderly man, who had a crescent-moon-shaped pale face and blue eyes. She told him all about her son's discovery. However, as she could observe, for someone Edward's age, he was very fortunate to have his vision still strong. He kept that long gray goatee he had grown, which went well with his emerald waistcoat and silver pocket watch.

The pocket watch was special. It had the ability to project past events that took place among the council from years ago so they could learn from their mistakes. For a moon-man, he could get easily frustrated when it came to important business among the council members with rules not being followed.

Terri nodded. "I beg your pardon for disturbing you, but I and my husband have come with bad news."

"Oh really?" Edward said. "This should be interesting. Tell me. What has brought you to the council, disturbing me in the middle of the night?"

"This," Terri said as Tom stepped forward, reaching into his pocket and pulling out the stone he carried. He held out the demonic stone inside the palm of his hands to show it to Edward, who was now sitting on his rocker upon the balcony. It gave him a good view.

"My son found this inside our jewelry business," Tom said.

Edward's eyes blinked twice. He couldn't make out the rock. "What is it? I can't see it. It's too far from me."

"A demonic rock," explained Terri.

"A demonic rock? Are you serious?"

Terri nodded.

Edward then said, "Stay right where you are. I will send out my assistant, who will come and hand it to me."

"Your assistant?"

Edward turned around and began to push down on a button. He spoke into a loud megaphone, imitating a T. rex's voice, "Christopher StompStomp, please come to my front yard immediately."

Tom groaned. He had forgotten. He didn't tell Terri yet.

Terri could see her husband groaning. "What's wrong?"

"StompStomp. I know what he is," Tom said.

"What is he?"

They could feel the ground beginning to shake, as if there was an earthquake. It made Terri and Tom wobble a couple of times on their feet, and they almost fell over. Before either of them could blink their eyes, something hopped quickly and loudly over the fence from Edward Cuddlebuggle's backyard. It was an enormous T. rex. He approached the front yard wearing a bowler hat on top of his head, giving him the semblance of being someone of importance.

"You called?" StompStomp said, catching his breath after giving Terri a friendly good-evening-ma'am tip with his black bowler hat. "It's half past midnight, Edward."

"I know," Edward said.

"You better have a good reason for this." StompStomp growled.

"I do. Trust me." Edward glanced down at Terri. "Can you please take that rock from Tom and hand it to me?"

StompStomp looked at Tom, who was holding the small demonic rock. He rolled his enormous black eyes as he snarled. He couldn't believe how much time he had wasted by running all the way over here. The things a T. rex does for his boss. This was stupid. He thought that Edward was only supposed to call him for major issues. "That is it? That's all you dragged me out of my nest for? Just to have me hand that stupid little rock over to you? Why couldn't you get off your own lazy bum from sitting in that chair and do it yourself?"

"I'm too old to make it down the stairs," Edward revealed. "I'm too tired and weak to climb back up and down. I don't have much pep in me as I used to, StompStomp. That's why you're my assistant and why I was given this paging system. It's for you to help me do things that are challenging for me."

"Fine. You know I do love you and the chicken sandwiches you reward me with. Not to mention the huge juicy steak you make me on the grill as my payment." StompStomp then took the demonic rock from Tom and handed it to his main man.

Edward took a good look at the stone. His eyes blinked twice. "Wowie, zowie."

"How much is Wowie, zowie?"

"I'm not talking about money. I am speaking from observing the relic." Edward held the stone up to the moonlight. He could see that the moon phases revealed some kind of odd code that only a boy spared by a wolf spirit could decode. "It gives me a reminder about something important. Something having to do with your son."

"My son?" Terri cocked an eyebrow. "What does Andrew have anything to do with this?"

"Is he with you?" Edward asked, not even answering her question as to why Andrew had anything to do with what he was observing. "Because it's time."

"Time for what?"

"Don't you remember? Back to the time and day of his birth. That one cold autumn night during an orange moon ceremony."

Terri had to think back to her son's birth. It was late in September. She recalled seeing Edward Cuddlebuggle when her son started doing odd things. He couldn't settle at night and was displaying very strange behaviors. He was climbing up walls and all over the furniture during his hyperactive impulses. It was like he was searching for something around the house. She didn't know what it was, but he looked everywhere for it. He was only about a year old. She then recalled asking her son, "Andrew, what are you looking for?"

"The white wolf," Andrew had said. "She comes out and plays with me at night, Mom."

The white wolf, Terri knew, was a legendary guardian spirit who looked out for another little boy many years ago. Way before the birth of her son. She asked Edward, "Is my son the boy under the watchful eye of the white wolf?"

"Indeed." Edward nodded, noting Terri's shock about her son being watched by a white wolf. "The white wolf was a guardian here. I knew from my prediction that, somehow, your son is a special boy. He's really special because of the orange moon ceremony. Please bring him to us. You'll see what I mean."

"But we have company," Terri began. "It would be rude to him right now, especially with there being a girl around."

"The girl who is with him may come," Edward said with a smile. "She's a princess, isn't she?"

"Yeah. Lauren," Terri said. "But how do you seem to know about her?"

"That is not to be a concern," Edward said. "Please bring them here immediately. I have a gift for your son, and I believe Lauren will love it." He snapped his fingers as the sound of drumbeats similar to an Indian drum began echoing through the walls. A group of butterflies came out into the clearing carrying a special box. It had an incredible gold color and small white crystal tips in each corner molded into dragonflies from the dragonfly forest.

"What's in there?"

"I will show you when you bring your son to me," Edward ordered.

Terri turned to Tom. "Go get the kids."

Tom did not have much choice in getting Andrew involved with their meeting with Edward Cuddlebuggle, nor did he think they needed to bring Lauren along. *Wait until Pumpkin and Tigger hear about this.*

"I will go get him and the princess," Tom said as he dashed right out the door. Terri stayed behind with Edward Cuddlebuggle.

Neither of them had noticed from above the ceiling of the glass dome as Tom made his way out, but the same little boy who threw the rock and broke their glass window was there. He was good at hiding and listening in on conversations, and he was shaking his head in disagreement about Andrew being given a gift.

That should be me receiving that crystal. I hate everything about her son, who I can tell is an android and not the real Andy. And I hate everything about that princess in the prophecy which was told to us as children. Dante was sending his minions who followed him in order to kill that boy of Terri's, including the princess who survived her kingdom's explosion. They both should've died, but it wasn't successful because of that blasted wolf spirit sparing both of their lives.

The boy wrestled with his thoughts as he felt the rage growing inside his fiery blue eyes. However, what was there to do now? How could he get that crystal? He could not with those witnesses around, especially after he threw one of the rocks.

The boy had decided he might as well wait when the coast was clear and nobody was watching the box. That would be the perfect time for him to snatch it and figure out how to harness its powers.

Those powers the crystal possessed were supposed to fill anyone with the knowledge needed to summon the darkness of the world and open the perils of hell believed to be nonexistent by many. It was the key to controlling the dimensions of the universe. He would love to have the power to manipulate them, which would make him a very powerful person.

Then he heard StompStomp say, "Allow me to take the box for safekeeping until Tom returns with those two special children."

Chapter 8

Lauren was still asleep. The only one who was still awake in bed was Andrew, who was staring out from his window at the village below. He sighed all over again, for he could not put it out of his mind.

That demonic rock, thrown on this very night at his family's store window, did a number of great concerns to him. Luckily, he was grateful nothing more serious than this had come, and it felt like this was only the beginning. Behind him, Pumpkin stood at his bedroom door.

"Andrew, aren't you able to sleep?" Pumpkin asked.

Andrew glanced over his shoulder to see the orange cat leaning against the door with arms crossed. "No." And then he returned his attention to gaze some more at the quiet and still streets as the rest of the town remained asleep outside his bedroom window. "I cannot sleep a wink. How can I after someone wrecked my folks' shop?"

Pumpkin could sense through his whiskers the underlying fear Andrew was hiding beneath his anger. He could understand the phobia of being hurt—not just by a rock breaking a shop window but by anything. He strolled over to stand beside the boy and take a look at the lands beyond the village with him. He scratched a claw behind his right ear before speaking again. "You know you're not the only one who has been hurt."

Andrew raised an eyebrow. "I know I'm not, and I never thought that. What makes you think I am?"

"By the way you're not getting your good night's rest and how you're staring down at the boys who are passing us and preparing to blow up Silly String cans," Pumpkin said, pointing a finger toward a group of boys who were laughing their entire heads off nearby as they were blowing up Silly String cans. "If I don't say any better, those boys must be good friends of yours."

"Well, I do know them. However, I don't hang out with them. They aren't exactly friends of mine. I spend most of my time alone when I blow up Silly String cans," Andrew said, going back to bed and allowing his head to hit the pillow. He knew those boys would never include him.

"Well now." Pumpkin then started to encourage the boy to keep on talking with interest twinkling in his green eyes. "Maybe one of those boys has something to do with that rock smashing through your window? Is there anyone you know who resides close to you who might have done this?"

Andrew closed his eyes. He imagined an earlier period in his life. Since his mother left his biological father, nothing had been the same. He did love Tom, who was a wonderful stepfather to him and a loving husband to his mother. However, his real father—well, that was a whole 'nother story. He knew for certain, whoever did this was holding something against him, and he would like to meet them. He said, "Look, I really don't have any idea on who threw that rock. Why don't we just drop it for now." He then rolled over to the right and placed an arm around Lauren, who continued to sleep.

There was an unlocking sound coming from downstairs at the front door. It closed and the door was locked again. He could smell cologne.

"Obviously, it's Tom," Pumpkin said, closing his eyes. "I hope he's full of good news."

Pumpkin could see Andrew, who had finally fallen asleep with his glasses on. The orange cat went up to the boy and removed his bifocals, placing them down on the side table. He then tiptoed out of the bedroom. As he closed the door, he came face-to-face with Tigger coming up the staircase.

"Pumpkin," Tigger said as the orange cat finished closing the door behind him. "I was just coming to wake the kids. Tom's home."

"Oh man. Andrew had just drifted off to la-la land. He was having a hard time sleeping."

"That doesn't matter. Tom needs you to wake them up," Tigger informed him. "He needs to speak to both of them in the backyard. It's important."

Pumpkin grumbled a little to himself before opening the door again, allowing Tigger into the room. He watched as the loving tan cat walked across the room and placed a paw on Lauren's shoulder, shaking her gently. "Lauren. Come on, Lauren. Wake up."

Lauren crinkled her eyebrows as she said with half a yawn, "Ugh, mum-mum. It's the middle of the night. I am too tired to make cookies."

Tigger rolled his eyes. He shook her gently once again. "Lauren, come on. Get up. I am not your mother, and we aren't making cookies."

Lauren opened her eyes and began to stretch. She did not notice that when she stretched her arms out, she almost knocked her fist into Andrew's face.

Andrew's eyes snapped open as he said, "Watch it, Lauren. You almost bonked me in the nose."

Lauren turned to face Andrew with a sheepish grin. "I'm sorry, Andrew. It was an accident."

"Anyway, why are we getting up? I haven't gotten any sleep."

"Tom needs to speak with the two of you," Tigger informed them.

Speak with the two of us? Andrew's brows raised. It must be something to do with their meeting at Edward Cuddlebuggle's house.

"We might as well hop to it." Andrew stood up. "Come on, Lauren. I am looking forward to whatever Edward Cuddlebuggle has informed Tom about, even if I'd rather be catching a few Zs." Andrew got up along with Lauren, who still had a huge grin on her face. She tried to hold hands with him.

Andrew pulled his hand away. "Please don't hold my hand. I don't want your cooties."

Lauren furrowed her eyebrows. "Cooties. I don't have cooties. If I did, I wouldn't have slept in your bed with you. Which, by the way," she repeats, "It is really nice of you, Andrew, to allow me to sleep in your bed."

Andrew felt as if he could've struck himself in the face for it. He had forgotten Lauren had crawled into his bed before he could say anything to her. He quickly shook it off and said, "Look, it's nothing. We're nothing more. Okay. You are a guest for now. I don't even know you that well, and I prefer to keep it that way."

"Andrew," a warning call of his name came from Tom.

"It's no trouble, Andrew. I am fine with being a guest," Lauren said.

It was not a big deal to her. She was just thanking him for allowing her to stay for the night and not forcing her to sleep on the floor. They both began to head outside, where Tom had been waiting at a small table.

"What's up, Tom?" Andrew had a seat, and Lauren sat right next to him.

"Edward Cuddlebuggle told me to retrieve both of you and take you to his home," Tom said. "He has a gift for you, Andrew. He believes it's now time to tell you the truth of why your birth in September is important to your family."

Andrew didn't think it was going to be a discussion about his birthday. It was quite surprising. There must be more to it besides the regular old-fashioned "Happy birthday, Andrew!" which they had celebrated a while ago. Andrew then asked his stepfather, "Is that what this meeting is about? Wishing me a happy birthday again?"

"No, Andrew, no. Please listen without cracking a joke. This meeting is serious business this time. Edward Cuddlebuggle is grateful your mother and I had brought the demonic rock you discovered to his attention. You and Lauren are invited to his place to discuss further more about the event of the rock being thrown at our window," Tom said, glancing at Lauren.

"That's great, Tom," Andrew said, full of energy. "Why don't we go now? Edward Cuddlebuggle may do something fun that's risky-frisky!" He began rushing to the door with a goofy, excited grin on his face only to come to a surprise stop when Tigger grabbed him by his shirt collar from behind.

"Not so fast, Eager McBeaver," Tigger said, keeping him from running to jump over their fenced-off yard. Andrew wanted to get ahead of everyone heading toward Edward Cuddlebuggle's home.

"And I don't believe that," Tom said, remembering the discussion Edward Cuddlebuggle had with him and Terri earlier tonight. "The old man seems cautious for a frisky type."

Andrew raised a brow. "Since when is Edward very cautious? He's usually excited when new guests come to the village. Maybe things are different this time, and he's being a bit sensitive."

"Trust me, Andrew. Edward Cuddlebuggle has been waiting for this day for the past twelve years," Tom said, giving a hint on what was to come for his stepson as he stepped out. He then unlocked the gate to their backyard as Pumpkin, Tigger, and Lauren followed him from behind.

"Twelve years?" Pumpkin wondered as he crossed his arms. "Is my hearing okay, Tigger, or am I a bit hard of hearing? Is there something we're missing?"

"No. You've heard correctly, Pumpkin," a voice said, disrupting the group's discussion on the matter. "Your ears have not lost their ability to listen." They turned to glance at the speaker who addressed them.

Andrew couldn't see anyone close by. He then said, "That was weird. Anyway, why don't we finish our discussion at Edward Cuddlebuggle's house? I would love to hear the rest of the story."

"But who was that voice speaking?" Pumpkin asked.

"I don't know. It doesn't matter. Come on. Edward Cuddlebuggle is waiting!"

The group of friends began to head straightaway to Edward Cuddlebuggle's home.

In the grass below the patio, sitting upon a rock, was a dwarf hamster who remained unnoticed. He had silver fur and held a small gold badge upon his blue cloak, which gave him the authority of being one of the rodent members. He was standing there with his beady black eyes recalling having met Andrew from somewhere.

No matter. He might as well follow the trio to Edward Cuddlebuggle's home as well, considering he had finished investigating the shattered window at the jewelry shop. He had become incredibly curious about the demonic rock. He didn't see that being part of his evidence. He began to scurry down through the grass like he was following a dirt path deep within a grassy forest.

Chapter 9

Terri pushed Edward Cuddlebuggle in his wheelchair as they made their way through the long and narrow corridors of his home. He was pondering over his town and the reason he requested for Andrew and Princess Lauren to be brought right to him.

"I cannot wait to see the look on Andrew's face when we give him his gift," Edward Cuddlebuggle said as he watched Terri admiring the colorful orbs lighting up the halls. These made the darkness shrink in every corner of the hallway as she pushed him toward the greenhouse part of his home.

This is where Edward Cuddlebuggle had the crystal of wisdom stored. As Terri wheeled him closer, he could sense its presence as the fireflies lit up the way to his garden room, showing off the plants inside. These were known as the Laurentum flowers, where the name *Lauren* was brought into existence. At the end of the room, there was a statue of a white wolf holding on to the box containing the crystal. It was the same box Terri had seen with Tom before he had left to go and retrieve her son.

"Edward Cuddlebuggle," a voice whispered from behind him.

Edward glanced over his shoulder to see StompStomp standing behind him, peeking through the side window with one of his big green eyes.

"I just saw Tom," StompStomp reported. "He has returned with the kids."

"I cannot wait to see the look on Andrew's face when we give him this crystal," Edward repeated with excitement. "Let them inside my home. Tell them to meet me at my indoor greenhouse."

"Right away," StompStomp said as he began to run toward the front door, making the family portraits inside the halls shake as he passed by them.

After the T. rex left, Edward Cuddlebuggle stood up from his wheelchair to stretch while waiting for his other guests of honor to join them.

Terri then asked, "Besides the crystal and Laurentum flowers, what else do you have inside your little house here?"

"A variety of different plants," Edward Cuddlebuggle replied, "especially chia pets."

"Chia pets?" Terri looked over her shoulder to see Andrew coming. He was dashing down the hallway with Lauren following behind along with Tom, who looked as if he was about to give them a warning about running in the hallway. You could hurt yourself or knock something over.

"I spend a lot of time with chia pets. I have a few at my house in my backyard."

"Then you're definitely worth giving the gift I'm going to give to you," Edward Cuddlebuggle said. And then as Andrew approached, he said, "I'm so glad to have finally met you, my grandson."

"Grandson?" Andrew looked questioningly at Terri.

"Yes, Andrew. This is your grandfather, Edward Cuddlebuggle," Terri said. "He was with us during the time of your birth twelve years ago during the orange moon ceremony."

Orange moon ceremony? Twelve years ago, that is exactly what Tom said back at their house, at their discussion inside the backyard. What do these pieces of the puzzle mean? Andrew wanted to know more. "What does this all mean?"

Andrew couldn't help feeling a little dazed and confused about where his grandfather was heading with this. He began to see his grandfather admiring Lauren as she stuck a hand out to shake his, so he barely heard his grandson's question.

"Ah, you must be Princess Lauren, who arrived a while ago and became friends with Andrew," Edward said.

"She's not my friend. She's a guest," Andrew began to correct his grandfather, but Tom only ruffled his hair.

"Oh, you're such a kidder," Tom said dismissively with a wave of his hand as he could see the grandfather wasn't seeing any humor in Lauren not being a friend but just a visitor that's just passing on through. "Trust me, Lauren. He's joking. Don't mind him. Andrew's kidding around. Otherwise, you wouldn't have introduced yourself after that little bump you had with him."

"I'm not kidding. Let's get to the gift you want to give me," Andrew demanded impatiently.

"Andrew," scolded Terri, scowling at her son's rudeness. His rudeness has been off and on earlier in the afternoon. She looked at her father remorsefully. "I'm sorry."

"It's fine," Edward said as he began to punch in the combination to the greenhouse once again, making the statue accept the code. And it began to slide to the right "The gift is inside here, hidden within those chia pets."

They began to head into the greenhouse, and as they did, the teenage boy who threw the demonic rock at the store appeared again. He had seen how Edward Cuddlebuggle had accessed the greenhouse to get it to move out of their way. Now he knew how to give it a go.

So they think the crystal is secured here, eh? Well, not secure enough to stop me from snatching it, he thought to himself. *Edward Cuddlebuggle is doing foolish thinking that a greenhouse with some combination could keep me from that crystal. He is pathetic. And it's disappointing to see Lauren in overalls.* The teenage boy was changing his mind about Lauren. If she was a princess, then where was her crown and dress?

He then looked over toward Andrew with a little confusion. *I don't get why Lauren would want to be with Andrew. She's so naive and doesn't realize he's made up of metal, wires, and electricity. Also, his appearance is hideous and man-made, with a weird recording for his voice. Thank God her aunt Debbie likes me better than him and wants her to be with someone as handsome as me because I am much more handsome and more normal than other guys around. She would not want her with this disgusting-looking, weird nutcase boy made up of scrap metal. I mean, Lauren and I would be perfect for each other. She loves having her way like me. I succeed all the time at getting my way, especially when it comes to creating mischief for others, and they get the blame for everything I did. As I had said in my message to them on that demonic rock I shot at Andrew's window, there's always happy moments in misery. That's something I'd love to contribute to this world.*

Andrew gazed around at the chia pets. There were many covering shelves, hanging up from the ceiling, and on tables. The final chia pet he noticed was a fake white wolf statue with roses growing from it.

"Roses." Lauren smirked as her eyes sparkled, her nose ready to smell the scents. "What a beautiful garden you have here, Mr. Cuddlebuggle."

"Why, thank you, Princess," Edward said. "I and my assistant worked hard to keep it nice. It's hard, however, with the weeds growing everywhere and…" He then trailed off and couldn't help getting distracted from the topic at hand after seeing and hearing Lauren taking a big whiff of the roses and Andrew fiddling around with the chest containing the crystal. The boy was struggling with it. "Having trouble with the lock?"

"Yes. How do you get this blasted thing open?" Andrew questioned with the irritation growing in his eyes.

"You have to say a certain prayer," Edward Cuddlebuggle revealed.

"What kind of prayer?"

"A prayer belonging to the white wolf," Edward Cuddlebuggle said. "I know it by heart. Allow me. Stand back."

Andrew stepped away from the chest that held the crystal, allowing Edward Cuddlebuggle to approach it. He watched the old man get down on his knees and recite the prayer ahead of them. "O mighty white wolf, with fur as white as snow, you have chosen an ugly-smart boy under an orange-moon glow. He is shining with beauty under his appearance from head to toe. You grant him the gift of protecting the princess from every foe. He is her guardian angel. This is so."

The chest holding the crystal made a beeping sound of acceptance from its shielding sensor. The top of the chest opened, allowing a radiant glow to come shining through, which almost blinded everyone.

"Man! That's bright," Terri said.

The old man had noticed everyone behind him covering their eyes, and he began to head straight toward the wall where there was a shelf. He kept special glasses there, and he grabbed about six of them. He then said, "Put these glasses on. They'll protect your eyes from blindness."

The group did as they were told, placing the special crystal glasses on. Edward Cuddlebuggle grabbed the sky-blue diamond inside, which was lying upon a cushion.

"Is this what you wanted to give me?" Andrew asked as he stepped forward to accept the gemstone.

"Yep. This is for you to behold the crystal of wisdom," Edward said. "It's from the white wolf herself. She created the stone. You totally deserve it, my dear grandson." He turned to look at Terri. "You should be honored, Terri. Andrew and this wolf have known each other for a long time."

The teenage boy—who had been watching Andrew take the stone from his grandfather—remained hidden in the shadows. He watched Andrew become the guardian angel of Princess Lauren.

He was peering down, barely smiling, and sitting in silence as he gritted his pearly white teeth with frustration. He needed to leave. He could not take this anymore.

Andrew held the crystal in his hands as he turned to face his folks and three new allies. Then all of a sudden, the crystal in his hands began to crackle with electricity. It was a very strong force. It had picked up on both his and the princess's spiritual indigo aura, which existed within both their hearts and souls. It made the boy lose his grip on it as it split itself in half.

"What is happening?" Lauren asked.

"I don't know," Edward Cuddlebuggle said. He didn't think any crystal was supposed to do this. He watched along with the others, and their jaws dropped at the sight of both halves of the crystal changing into two necklaces.

The first necklace went around Lauren's neck magically, and the other did the same to Andrew as well. They then noticed the electrical light begin to fade, signaling the completion of the wisdom crystal's transformation.

Lauren glanced down and witnessed her necklace contained rainbow colors, and it was in the shape of a shard. As for Andrew, his was a shark's-tooth necklace.

That's it? That's my gift? Seems a lame one to give me and Princess Lauren, Andrew thought to himself.

Lauren furrowed her eyebrows as she said out loud, "It's not a lame gift, Andy!"

Andrew looked at Lauren in shock. How did she know he was thinking the crystal of wisdom gave them a lousy souvenir?

He decided to say something. He opened his mouth but then closed it again. He couldn't find the words.

Terri noticed and asked, "Are you all right?"

"Oh, Andy's perfectly fine, Terri," Lauren said. "He's just shocked. I can hear his thoughts."

Andrew tried to do the same thing back to Lauren. He could hear her think, *Hooray! I stumped him. Score 1 for girls.*

Andrew then said, "Hey! You don't need to keep score!"

Lauren realized he heard her thoughts. "Andrew, you just read my mind."

Andrew's cheeks flushed as he said, "You're right."

Pumpkin then said to Edward, "Eddy, could you explain to us what exactly is going on?"

Edward shrugged. "Um…I don't know. Maybe telepathy is one of the gifts the crystal gave those kids."

Telepathy? Lauren and Andrew looked at each other for a few minutes. *Is that even possible?* They just heard each other's thoughts together at the same time.

Lauren then realized something—something she had recalled from her kingdom. A memory came back to her at the mention of telepathy. She felt herself becoming uneasy as she began to slump to the ground.

Andrew had taken notice and bent down next to her. "What's wrong?"

Lauren didn't answer. The pupils in her brown eyes, once wide, began to shrink as if they had come into the sunlight for the first time after being trapped inside a dark cavern. She could hear something— laughter coming from above them near the ceiling.

"Don't you hear that?" Lauren asked.

"Hear what?"

"Shh. Be quiet and listen," Lauren said.

Andrew did as he was told, and very faintly, he could hear laughter coming from the corridors. It sounded like some type of animal and some guy was fooling around the walls of Edward Cuddlebuggle's house. How peculiar.

Chapter 10

A powerful gust blew through the house, making the garden within the room grow cooler. Lauren and Andrew rubbed their arms as they watched Edward Cuddlebuggle pull out his matches. He struck it, creating a flame. Shielding it from the air, he headed over to the small fireplace, avoiding things that could put the little fire-stick out. No hoses or buckets of water were left in sight, but he still could see a small puddle that was put out before on the concrete floorboards.

Edward then commanded, "Could someone go get a Wet Floor sign so anyone who has a lantern will be warned ahead?"

"I'll get it, Mr. Cuddlebuggle. We don't need anyone slipping or sliding. They will hurt themselves," StompStomp said as he left to grab the Wet Floor sign inside the supply closet down the hallway.

"I can't believe it," Andrew said.

"Believe what?" Lauren asked.

"This crystal has given us gifts," Andrew said.

"Oh, I thought it was something else you were going to tell me," Lauren said, shaking her head.

It didn't take long for the building to begin shaking violently, making everyone fall to the ground. It had become forceful enough to knock down the entire building from its structure.

"What is going on!"

"Everybody, don't panic," Pumpkin said, trying to calm the unsettling situation. "We're just caught in an unusual storm from… from…"

"Hell?" a dark voice completed the orange cat's sentence.

"Yes, thank you for finishing what I wanted to say, Tigger," Pumpkin said.

"Uh… Pumpkin, I didn't say anything," Tigger pointed out as he sat in the little room right next to the dusty old tables surrounding the statue of the white wolf with Edward Cuddlebuggle's chia pets. It had fallen, breaking into pieces and making a mess.

Pumpkin wasn't surprised by it. The same kind of incident happened at the Parrot Library. Now it was beginning to make more sense after receiving the message and witnessing the books swirl around Lauren.

"Not my chia pets! I've just grown those plants!" Edward Cuddlebuggle said, rather upset, as he banged a clenched fist on the side of the wall.

The walls of the teeny room they were in began to grow cracks and seep through as laughter came. They looked around frantically for whoever was chuckling in such an optimistic way.

Lauren was the first to address the voice with her remaining bravery, even if her voice had become small. "Who is there? If you're the person who has been stalking me and Andrew throughout Bad-Mouther's Brook, I demand you leave us both alone!"

The laughter became even stronger, causing Lauren to lose her courage and become frightened enough to hide behind Andrew, who stood there crossing his arms. He wasn't bugging an inch with his eyebrows furrowing. He was not at all impressed with the mystery guy's entrance and scaring the princess half to death. He put his arm around her protectively and said, "Don't worry. I will protect you."

"You promise?"

"I promise," Andrew said. "I will make sure you will always be safe."

Outside the room, the light bulbs in the hallway were surging, and the voice said, "Yes! Yes! Reveal all your phobias to me. For I am…" He paused for a bit. "For I am the dark master. For I am the one who opened the knowledge crystals. For I wooo!" He walked into a puddle on the ground, causing him to slide and come through the curtain door into the room where Andrew and the others stood. His hood fell from his head, revealing his true identity. It was the same boy with long brown hair and blue eyes. He quickly put his hood up to hide his identity; however, it was too late.

Lauren immediately recognized him, and she stopped herself from being afraid. Her fear became anger at the sight of him. "Hey! You're that boy who shot the demon rock at Tom's shop window."

"Of course I am. And I am here to tell you an important truth," the boy said.

"What truth?" Lauren questioned.

"That guardian angel who has that shark necklace isn't a real angel," the boy began. "He's nothing more than an illusion, including his family. They are nothing except a group of androids who have been lying to you."

Lauren looked at Andrew. "Are you really an android?"

"No. Don't be silly," Andrew told her. "I am not made up of metal, wires, or such nonsense. I wouldn't lie to you, Princess, in order to lower you into traps to kill you."

Lauren looked back at the boy. "You're the liar!"

The boy chuckled. He reached into his pocket to grab the slingshot he had. "Looks like I'm going to have to do this the hard way." And with his sapphire eyes filled with aggression similar to a shark swimming around a reef, he aimed at his target to give him a mighty bite. "Say goodbye to Andrew Cuddlebuggle."

Andrew felt his eyes grow all steely as he found himself going into defense mode, which was what the boy was expecting from him. He wanted him to do that. He said as a repeat warning, "Stay away from the princess. You're the android!"

Andrew started running toward him just as the boy let go of his slingshot, shooting a rock in the shape of an android-killing bullet. It came flying and hit him smack-dab inside the chest, which created an electrical surge throughout his body. Andrew began shaking all over as he collapsed in front of the princess.

This made her eyes widen in amazement. She had been wrong. "That's impossible. Androids aren't supposed to exist, and yet they do," Lauren said in a teasing way.

A scream came from behind the princess. It was Terri, who came running over. "My baby! He has killed my baby!"

Terri could see with pretend panicked eyes the lifeless body of Andrew lying there as she approached him along with Tom. Another rock fired from the mysterious boy's slingshot hit them both in the chest as well, causing them to have the same reaction as Andrew had.

The mystery boy then said, after seeing her son lying there with his other followers, "I did, ma'am. I killed your son, who was an impostor similar to the rest of you. You are all pretending to be a family."

Edward has some explaining to do, Lauren thought to herself as she saw the professor, along with his dino assistant, trying to sneak away. She went right in front of them, blocking the door and keeping them from making an escape to the backyard, where he had a blimp waiting for him.

"Where do you think you're going?" Tigger asked Edward, who was coming up from behind him with Lauren and the mysterious boy close behind.

"Uh…I eh, you see…" Edward said, not sure on how to answer them. It was clear the old man was now quite startled.

"Tell us about this android family pretending to be a real family," Pumpkin demanded as he began to fidget impatiently with his fingers. "Tell me. I'm waiting."

Edward realized he had no choice. He swallowed hard as he made a confession. "I did. I made those androids as ordered by the dark one named Thor, the dragon of lightning."

"Edward Cuddlebuggle, you are under arrest," a yellow foxy lady declared, suddenly appearing after the old man's confession. She seemed to be a descendant from the Egyptian period. Her eyelids were covered with glittering purple eyeshadow, and she wore an outfit similar to that of a pirate's. There was a gold amulet containing a huge amethyst hanging down by her breast. It wonderfully complemented her violet eyes.

"Well, well, well." Edward growled as she arrested him. "We meet again, Sorphina. And you are still a sneaky double-crossing—"

"Oh, I'm double-crossing?" Sorphina said with her loud voice echoing through the house. "You're the one who double-crossed the princess with that phony family you had made up." She began patting down his pants for anything else he could be hiding. She felt two things in his pockets. She smiled. "Jackpot. I knew it was here. I knew you took priceless things from me." She reached into his pocket. She had discovered a booklet and three bottles of liquid.

The small booklet, Lauren could see, apparently had information about an island called "The Lost Luggage." That must be where Edward Cuddlebuggle had gotten the three bottles filled with black liquid, which were meant to be used by doctors for muscle-testing practices during the colonial times. She witnessed the foxy lady's temper rising as she began to integrate the old-man.

"Hey, give them back." Edward snarled. "I was using that to power my androids." He then realized he let his tongue slip as the foxy lady grinned.

"Really?" Sorphina said with a chuckle. "How interesting. Are there any more of those androids you built?"

"I don't quite—" Edward began, nearly choking on his tongue as he felt the foxy lady's paws and nails almost strangling him as she dug into his neck. His face had gone from white to a black-and-blue color due to his neck being squeezed. "I...don't...remember." His eyes were almost shut when he heard Lauren scream at the top of her lungs to the foxy lady.

"Stop it!" Lauren shouted, her eyes widening with horror. "You're killing him, Sorphina!"

The foxy lady let go, allowing Edward Cuddlebuggle to rub his neck as he fell to the floor. His legs could no longer hold him up due to the lack of oxygen and his blood pressure becoming low.

"Why, all of a sudden, do you care about android creators?" Sorphina seemed disturbed by the princess's sympathy for Edward, who stole from her. "He's from the shadow worlds. He is helping the fearsome creature you never ever ever want to meet. He will hurt you. He is capable of murdering—"

"I'm sorry, Sorphina," Lauren said with eyes filled with remorse. "I just can't stand to see anyone killed, including bad guys who break laws. There has to be better ways to handle the guilty who do wrong rather than strangling them to death."

"Bless you for it," Edward stated, impressed with the princess as he tried to stand up only to fail. He dropped to the ground and passed out.

"He's dying! You killed him, Foxy!" the mysterious boy said with hatred growing in his eyes.

"I didn't kill him," Sorphina muttered. "He's just unconscious for now. He'll wake up later. Why don't we get him on my ship to the Land of the Lost Luggage—that's my town—and continue from there when he awakens."

Lauren felt as if she was going to cry. Pumpkin, who sensed the princess's despair, came up to her and placed his arm around her. This only made her swat it away. She didn't feel like being hugged at the moment.

Pumpkin spoke gently to her, "Lauren, let it go. He is a suspect of a crime committed, and Sorphina and this mystery boy are doing their jobs."

Lauren wiped one more tear away and then came to face the orange tabby cat. He could see she was still upset about seeing the old man being strangled. So he did what he could do. He opened his arms, and she gave in to hugging him. He gazed over the princess's shoulder at the foxy-lady, the mysterious boy, and Tigger going around and gathering all the evidence that had been left behind.

The boy ended picking up the small bottles Edward had in his pocket. There was some fine print on them with an X below the word *Wormwood*. Tigger turned it around and noticed there was information about them and who they belonged to.

It read, "If you happen to find these bottles lost, be careful with them. They are filled with strong magical ingredients mixed together by two crazy griffin ladies who are the owners of a shop close to a bridge they guard with their life. These two ladies' names are Georgia Pomegranate and Peggy Entwistle, residing inside the Island of the Lost Luggage."

Lauren let go of Pumpkin and walked over to the android lying on the ground. She could see a part of him peeling off from the face. She began to strip the face off. As she did, she found it very elastic and rubbery in texture. Underneath it were lots of wires and stuff, as expected, including a voice box with a built-in speaker. It kept on saying its lines repeatedly, "My name is Andrew." It did this more than three times in a row.

"Well, I thought he was real," Lauren said. And she thought he was almost her first friend around here. She couldn't believe she allowed her naivety to take over once again. She then saw the shark's-tooth necklace around the android's neck. She went to take it away from the android as the mysterious boy approached her from behind.

"We're sorry, Lauren. You see, I had to, you know," the boy said with a little empathy. He could sense the princess didn't know that this was a joke to pull.

Lauren sighed, taking a deep breath in, before getting mad. She dismissed the mystery boy. "You proved me wrong. I stand corrected. I wasn't very smart. I allowed my naivety to get to me."

"It's forgiven. Anyway, I didn't get a chance to fully introduce myself to you," the mystery boy said. "My name is Zack."

"Zack?" Lauren cocked an eyebrow. "Zack what?"

"Zack Renders," he finished.

"Beautiful name," Lauren said, admiring him a little.

Zack said, puffing up his chest with pride, "The name *Zack* stands for a beautiful city called Zackhak, home of the visual arts." He watched as Lauren took the shark necklace away from the android he put out of commission.

She turned to him and handed him the shark's-tooth necklace. "Do you want this?"

"No, you keep the necklace. Sharks aren't my favorite," Zack said. "Especially when they rip apart their prey."

Lauren had never thought of it before, but Zack's eye color, which was a sapphire blue, made him amazing. His eyes were the part she found most admirable about him. Speaking of that, she wondered if Zack knew anything. Does the city of Zackhak have any sort of connections? "Can you take me to the city of Zackhak?" she asked.

Zack scratched his chin, thinking over what Lauren had just asked him. "Why would you want to go there?"

"To know more about the white wolf," Lauren said, pointing to the statue behind her inside the garden-room part of the building.

Zack could see the others moving out of the way to give him more of a good view of the white wolf statue. He thought it over, and he said, "I could take you. But first things first so you are aware the city isn't the friendliest. Nor is it the most normal place in the world."

"Not friendly? Not normal? Can you explain more?"

"It's a well-known home to the notorious Squid Boys who roam the streets," Zack informed the princess. "They're a super dangerous and a very strong gang. I was part of a gang at some point in my life when I had an encounter with them."

Squid Boys? They sounded rather strange for a bunch of thieves. However, it was disheartening to hear how Zack had been part of a gang at some point. She didn't know if this was a good influence for him. Also, this could bring death to them. Zack was a survivor from a jumping incident.

Lauren reached over and patted Zack on the shoulder. "I'm glad you're alive. You did what you had to do to survive. Anyway, is that where you got that slingshot you used to kill off that robotic family? Do they carry such weapons?"

Zack shook his head. "No. I made that slingshot as a way to protect myself since I lived inside a rough area. I'm innovative. I made other things besides it, hoping to earn back the same amount of money they took from me during the jumping. Money I owe to one of my teammates."

"We might as well get going," Pumpkin interrupted them. The two boys were no longer mysterious. However, they were now considerably strange and pretty goofy.

Pumpkin came over with Tigger and Sorphina following him as he caught the princess's attention. He could see the sun beginning to come up and peek through the paint-stained windows of Edward Cuddlebuggle's house, and he felt himself growing rather sleepy from being up most of the night and having lots of this stuff happening. "We need to get to our next stop from here. We got the crystal of wisdom."

"Pumpkin, if you're too tired, I can drive us to the next stop," Sorphina said as she began to lift Edward Cuddlebuggle off the floor. She then made her way toward the entrance of his home. She was going to take him to her ship in order to continue her interrogation, where the rest of the pirates were waiting.

"Thank you for the offer, Sorphina. However, I would rather drive myself and my friends. I will just grab a cup of warm milk to keep me awake," Pumpkin said. "You should get ahead of us to the Lost Luggage Island."

"Suit yourself. Come along, Eddy," Sorphina said. She grunted as she carried him out of the house.

Sorphina could hear Edward mumble as he stayed in dream mode, "Don't call me Eddy." She made her way out to the docks of Bad-Mouther's Brook where her boat was parked.

Lauren began to leave with the others, following behind the foxy lady. She could see StompStomp still standing there with his arms crossed. He was peering over at the picture frames on the walls. She then said to Zack, "Would you excuse me for a minute?"

"It's no trouble," Zack said. "I will wait outside for you with the others."

Lauren went back to StompStomp, who was straightening out the picture frames that had been knocked crooked from the intrusion. One of the picture frames was of him hatching from his egg in front of Edward Cuddlebuggle.

"Is that you?" Lauren asked.

"Yep, that's me," StompStomp said. "Me being hatched inside Edward Cuddlebuggle's lab, right before he created the android family." He smiled, showing off his pearly white carnivorous teeth as he chuckled to himself. He was back at that moment in time. It was one of his best memories. "I was something then for a hatchling."

He watched the princess peer at the other photographs along the walls.

Each photograph told a story. One of them had StompStomp more grown up and wearing a black suit as he stood outside Edward Cuddlebuggle's house. It was night, and he was waiting to take some letters across the lands to summon all the other scientists around the realms. They had come near and far to see the androids Edward had created. It was during a time when it was not considered illegal to make androids in their worlds, as it was right now.

StompStomp frowned. It was a shame that Edward Cuddlebuggle had now been taken into custody by Sorphina and the other pirates.

"Are you coming or what?"

Lauren and StompStomp looked over at Zack, who was leaning against the front door, waiting for them.

"I'd better go. It looks like Zacky is becoming antsy inside his pantsy," Lauren said. She could see StompStomp extend one of his teeny arms out to her.

"It's been nice meeting you, Princess Lauren. I wish you luck finding the other crystals," StompStomp said.

"Aren't you coming?"

"No, I'd rather stay. Keep the house until Edward Cuddlebuggle returns," StompStomp said.

"Come on, Lauren." Zack came up to Lauren and grabbed her by the hand. She looked at his face, and he looked a little irritated. Obviously, he has got to learn to have a little more patience because she didn't like him dragging her right out the door.

"Can you please stop pulling me?" Lauren growled. "I understand we have to go."

"Yeah, but you were taking too long," Zack said with annoyance. "So you gave me no other choice but to drag you out of the house."

As they made their way out of the building, StompStomp pushed a button to close the double doors behind the children. He watched them move down the staircase with the bright sun shining right into Lauren's and Zack's eyes.

Lauren covered herself; the sun stung. She felt as if she just had come out of an extremely dark cavern she was trapped inside after some horrible explosion out of nowhere. It was the same feeling she recalled having when her castle went down in pieces after it got destroyed. She noticed, not too far ahead, the foxy lady placing Edward Cuddlebuggle in the back of her boat. The boat wasn't huge nor incredibly small. It was medium-sized and had enough room to take everyone to the next destination.

The boat had really unique tiki-Western qualities, which gave it tropical and Wild West features, especially with the fake parrots with bull horns sticking through their heads. She had never seen a tropical Wild West theme. She guessed maybe things were always weird on Lost Luggage Island. She could see the ship's name: *The Foxy-Poxy*.

Lauren's thinking was interrupted when she heard an engine roaring. The same roar she would recognize when Pumpkin started the Boot-Hoot. That means the cats must've gone to get their vehicle parked out in front of the impostors' house, close to the three-pointed signs she had seen prior to their arrival at this town.

Lauren breathed in and out as she walked down toward the docks. She could see Sorphina had finished placing Edward Cuddlebuggle inside the back of her boat, where she kept her prisoners.

"Is he awake yet?" Lauren asked as she could see Sorphina struggling to close the back of the boat.

"Not yet," Sorphina said, finally getting the back door of the boat to close.

"Those edges need oiling," Lauren pointed out. They looked rusty.

Pumpkin then bopped her up against the head. "Knock it off."

"I was just saying it needs oiling," Lauren said. "And aren't we riding with them to the next island?"

"No. We're taking the Boot-Hoot," Pumpkin said. As he looked across the ocean, he could see a bridge cutting across toward the next land. The bridge was very large and red, and it had lanterns with human eyes that blinked once or twice as vehicles passed on by.

"Man, I wanted to ride with them," Lauren said with a little pout to her face.

Sorphina then got down to Lauren's eye level. She understood how she felt on ride-alongs. She was like that sometime in her life as a fox-kit. She had more of an understanding now as an adult, so why not share them for various reasons? "Hey, you need to listen to Pumpkin," the fox lady told her. "Our way of travel is rather rough, and it can become hazardous. Too hazardous for a princess."

"Okay," Lauren said. She wondered why they thought traveling with them would be too chaotic for her. She was already on this journey to find the crystals. It made her cross her arms. They had poor judgment.

"Come on, Lauren," Pumpkin called her. "Time to head back to the Boot-Hoot and get back on the road."

"I'm coming. Just give me a minute," Lauren said as she turned to look at Zack, who was putting his things inside the boat. She went up and tapped his right shoulder to gain his attention.

"What is it?" Zack turned to look Lauren in the eyes after straightening out his things.

"Um, I wanted to say…" Lauren suddenly felt nervous about what she wanted to say to Zack. She couldn't help but gaze at his sapphire-blue eyes.

"Goodbye?" Zack finished for her.

"Uh, yeah," Lauren said as she stuck her hand out to shake his. "It was my pleasure meeting you. Here."

"It was great to meet you too," Zack said, shaking hands with her. He then stepped onto the boat with Sorphina following him from behind. He began to take the boarding plank from the dock. After untying it from the dock, he heard the foxy-lady give orders to pull out. "We're set to go, Sorphina."

It didn't take long for hollering to come from behind Lauren. "Wait! Wait! I have something for Edward!"

StompStomp was running pretty fast from Edward's house on top of the hill, holding in his hands a brand-new business suit for the old man to wear. "He may want his business suit, for when you have a trial for him." He held it out to Zack—a black suit that came with black pants, black tie, black sneakers, and a white shirt to go with it. "You don't want him to stay in his dinosaur pajamas now, would you?"

The T. rex could see he wasn't going to make it in time, so he continued to run at a much quicker pace, only to find he still wasn't going to catch them in time. He slowed down so he wouldn't fall into the ocean. "Darn it! Am I too late?"

"I'm afraid so," Lauren said, watching with him as the boat left for the Land of Lost Luggage. She could see it departing from a good distance, straight into the sunrise coming over the ocean peak. "The group of random strangers and that very odd, mysterious, and handsome Zack went with them."

"That really sucks," StompStomp said. "I wanted to give them Edward's business suit, for when he wakes up. He will need it for the trial they're going to give him. It's not good to just show up to court inside your dinosaur-friendly pajamas."

Lauren kept staring off into space. She was barely listening to StompStomp complaining all about his master, who left with the group of strangers and not having the right clothes to wear. Her mind kept on churning, wandering back to the part where Zack mentioned something about him being the one who opened the knowledge crystals, the book that belonged to her family. What did he mean by that?

Pumpkin noticed her staring off into the horizon as Tigger calmed the T. rex down from his infernal complaining, which was driving him a little nuts.

"Can you please stop complaining, TR?" asked Tigger.

"Why should I?" StompStomp asked, shoving his face into Tigger's.

Tigger then grabbed him by his oversized head and turned it to show what he was talking about. Lauren was still watching the boat leave as Pumpkin joined her on the dock. She barely noticed him there.

"He really took my breath away," Lauren mumbled under her breath.

"Lauren," Pumpkin began, noticing her naiveness was starting to take hold. It was a sign a daydream was coming to play like a movie inside her mind. He could see she had a huge grin spreading across her face. He shook her gently. "Lauren. Come on, Lauren."

Lauren snapped out of it. "Huh? Wha?" The dream she had about her and Zack together disappeared, bringing her back to reality.

"Glad to have you back on earth," Pumpkin said as he went in front of her. "You need to stay away from Zack."

"What? Why? What's wrong with him, Pumpkin?" Lauren asked, her eyes shining with gratitude. "I was just thanking him for helping us." She couldn't quite understand what Pumpkin had against Zack. "He seems strapping. I admire the mystery he has about him, besides his name."

"Lauren, he wasn't helping us with anything." Pumpkin began to explain more to her by giving her a huge reality check. "You just met him. And besides, didn't he say he opened the knowledge crystals?"

Lauren barely heard anything Pumpkin was saying to her about Zack admitting to opening the crystals again. She was too deep in her daydream of being in love with him that she let him get away. She damned herself. "Darn! I should've grabbed his contact info. I didn't think of it."

"Lauren, are you listening?" Pumpkin asked her once more.

She looked at the orange cat, defeated. "Yeah, I heard you. He loves his sharks, slingshots, and…" Lauren trailed off. She really didn't feel like repeating what the orange cat had told her, but she thought she had better because his arms were crossed. "Pranks."

"That is not what I have said," Pumpkin said, rolling his eyes. The princess was right. Her memory wasn't too good. It was still foggy since they found her yesterday at their last camp out at Tortoiseshell Beach. Unfortunately, the android killing was the last thing Lauren could recall. "I don't know about him being your prince."

"Something you said about him loving to pull pranks," Lauren finished.

"Enough about that boy," Tigger interrupted them both as he opened the door to the Boot-Hoot. "We need to get going. We need to head to our next destination: the Land of Lost Luggage."

"Come on, Pumpkin," Lauren said as she began to put her crush on Zack behind her. "Let's keep on finding those crystals. I promise to be a little more careful."

Pumpkin tapped on the princess's shoulder, starting a race as Tigger had done with him out of the blue. "Let's all race back to the Boot-Hoot. If you get there, you're considered a stinky litter-box."

Then Pumpkin, Tigger, and Lauren began to run straight toward where the Boot-Hoot was parked. She began to pick up her pace, trying to keep up with the two cats. StompStomp just stood there wondering if he was supposed to be racing too.

He called out to them. "Hey, wait a minute!" He decided he had no other option but to go right after them. He went and chased after his friends. "I didn't even ask to start a race."

"Too bad, baggy-pants!" Pumpkin shouted after hearing Tigger's complaint.

Lauren laughed as they made their way to the Boot-Hoot. They climbed in and headed off to the Land of the Lost Luggage.

Chapter 11

The stream was still and silent within the scorched forest. Soon the air would be too smoky for anyone to breathe through and hot enough to scorch their skin when they met the eyes of flame.

Fire had devoured everything that had been built around this forest for the past few years. Everything that had been made of wood was now gone. Vanished. This created a great concern for the residents who remained behind. This great fire, ignited by a spark, could move faster than a person outrunning a deer, and it burned as if its leaping flames held a grudge against the world.

A girl who seemed to be older than fourteen appeared around the corner, barely grinning as her emerald eyes took in the view of the damage the fire had done. Under her arm, a crutch held her up as she kept looking all over for any survivors.

Her leg had apparently been broken due to the unfortunate event. Before she injured it, she had rushed into the swampy water after the boat her family owned. It came with their cabin, and when the boat had gotten loose and floated away from her, she dared to dive right in. She swam to it, believing she was alone. However, she wasn't alone for long inside the swamps. A crocodile managed to get ahold of her leg, scaring her half to death. She used her other leg to fight it off by kicking it forcefully in the face. She fought as hard as she could but only to fail. And when things seemed to look bleak, another croc appeared. It almost seemed the end for her when, suddenly, a spark of fire came from a pistol. It shot at both of the crocs, making them flee. She was left there close to drowning.

She felt something lift her from the water. And something began to carry her out of the water as she was losing consciousness.

She heard a soft voice saying, "Hold on. I've got you. You're going to be okay. I am taking you to a healer right away."

"Sori," a voice came from behind the girl, who had her gaze glued to the summertime sky as she watched birds fly off to the north of the forest. She came back to the present and turned to see a friend coming into view.

He was holding a brand-new knife in his hands. He lived on the street next to Sori and her relatives, on a street called Bleeker. After the fire, there were newer roads and houses built from scratch, and these didn't house many normal families. And at the end of the street, there was a sign representing a new institution: The Wailing Asylum.

"Did they let you out already, Nickels?" Sori questioned, cocking a brow when she heard him chuckle at the joke. It was quite obvious he had snuck out. She noticed the knife. "And cool dagger."

"Thanks. I used the $600 I had from my grandmother to buy myself a collection of these things that I now have in my room, stashed away, so Hale and Gale don't get their hands on them."

"You were wise," Sori said as she imagined what those two little demons would've done if they had discovered the knives lying around his hideout. "What are you doing out of the hospital?"

"I managed to sneak out with help."

"Who helped you?"

"Why, Lucifer of course," he told her. "You know how close we've been since I was a boy. We discovered we're not just boy and beast. We're more of a father and son. He's the type of father that takes me down a path that isn't so righteous, where I first came eye-to-eye with you, my friend." He touched Sori on the shoulder, making her flinch at the sensation of his cold hand. He stood there grinning devilishly, mischievous new plots coming to his mind.

Okay, yes. She had started out as his teammate, and she may have become a friend. However, deep down, she hated Lucifer.

If you're wondering about the Wailing Asylum, this trouble-making boy more likely had guts enough to escape than the others from their home, which kept them all together in one common group of the most abnormal, the most terrible, the most horrible, and the most weird creatures and people you wouldn't expect to discover on ordinary days. He was one of the strangest ones, especially with his ability to give off high-pitched, painful screaming.

Lucifer was the one who had given this special ability to the boy when he was a baby found inside a swampy area that was filled with crocodiles. It was during a time way before those crocodiles could've ripped Sori's arm and leg off, after her folks' boat got loose, and when the moon had sunk behind the trees, making them lower themselves into the muddy swamp, along with their shadows.

The boy was very grateful that the beloved remaining dinosaurs, which were known to be the dark master's guardians of the swamp, were willing to spare him. The two animals took him from the enormous mushroom cap which he rested upon inside the river covered with leaves. They were rather gentle with their mighty jaws, and they carried him to the devil himself as naturally as a mechanical stork with pixies controlling it flew through the sky. They delivered him straight to evil.

You'd think an infant similar to this boy would have been killed due to the fact that crocodiles had mighty jaws with sharp teeth. But no. Their dangerous teeth had no effect on him whatsoever. They delivered him straight to the Wailing Asylum, which a well-known woman named Georgia had created to house abandoned children.

A scream ripped through the forest. It awakened the ravens from their nests inside the oak trees surrounding Sori's house and made them scatter.

Sori could recognize that hollering from anywhere. It wasn't too hard.

Mercy! Sori thought to herself. It sounded as if she was in trouble. She looked around frantically for Nickel only to see he was halfway toward the river, where their canoes were docked.

Sori called to him. "Nickel, it's Mercy. I think she needs our help."

She heard Nickel chuckling to himself as he fixed his jet-black hair. She called out to him again. "Nickel, did you hear me?"

"Yes, Sori, I heard you," Nickel said. He continued to chuckle as he was walking away. *Like I really care that Mercy is having a complicated time at Wailing Asylum,* he thought to himself. *She's probably just having another one of her episodes. And besides, she has a roommate to settle her down.*

"Well, aren't you going to go back?"

Nickel turned around and began to walk backward while looking Sori straight in the eye. He said, "Mercy's problems aren't my problems."

Sori scowled at Nickel as he walked upon the small pier and untied the canoe. He hopped in to take it for a joyride.

She wished she had earplugs right now. That infernal screaming was driving her crazy. It was worse than a child going to the doctor's office to get the bunions on their tiny feet burned off.

She decided to walk right back into her home. She closed the door and limped all the way back to her bedroom. She made it to her bed, where she rested her crutch against the wall of her room. It didn't do much good. She could still hear the screaming coming through the thin old walls of her home. She would have to put up with it, so she decided to try and hide her head under her pillow. She could cover her ears with her chilled hands, and she closed her eyes tightly, praying that the hollering from the Wailing Asylum would be stopped by anyone who worked over there.

Sori knew Mercy had been dropped off there a week ago by her father. Mercy's father hated how she had dressed. She was very into punk rock, but really, he also knew for a fact that she loved listening secretly to K-pop and had boy-band posters all over the walls of their house.

Sori was certainly glad she wasn't anywhere near what Mercy was inside the asylum for. So who knew what went on within the asylum as she took a nap, as we speak.

Chapter 12

"Mercy, what's wrong?" Mythica—who was the screaming girl's roommate—asked. She had just returned from the bathroom after brushing her teeth. She resembled a pixie. You could tell by the beauty of her hazel eyes, peach skin, and light brown hair, which was cut into a bob. She was the older sister of a little brother who often came for a visit to the asylum.

"I had a weird dream," Mercy said, her jade-green eyes filled with concern.

Mythica groaned. "Do we have to do this now? I'm pooped."

Mercy could see Mythica was very tired after the day she had today. She had gone through electroshock therapy and would rather not hear a peep from her roommate about her strange illusions once again. She then looked at the small clock on the windowsill at the foot of her twin bed. She wished she could tell what time it was. It was too bad that the clock wasn't working right.

"I know you're tired, Mythica, but please listen to me," Mercy whispered. She shivered as a chill ran down her spine. "I have a feeling something is coming. A few visitors. Complete outsiders we've never met. There are two cats and a princess searching for crystals. They want to restore a kingdom."

Mercy then saw that Mythica had gone back to her bed across from hers. She was lying down on her back and staring up at the ceiling, repeatedly saying, "Why, oh why, do I have this psycho for a roommate? Someone who wakes you up to tell you every visionary thing they have every night. And those visionaries are pretty wacky. It's no wonder her father left her here. Two cats and a princess. Where does this roommate of mine even come up with or get all of these crazy ideas popping into her mind? I don't know how she can even sleep at night."

Mythica then heard Mercy persistently banging on their bedroom door. Her roommate had gotten out of bed and was now hollering for someone to come to their room.

"Hey! Nurses or anyone out there who is willing to evacuate us! It'll be great if you could warn the townsfolk of Lost Luggage that we're going to be in danger. There's a princess and two cats coming to take the crystal belonging to our island! Please, let me and the rest of the patients out of here!"

Then a feminine voice answered over the PA system, "Mercy Screams-a-Lot, it's time to settle down. Everyone is going to bed."

Tell me about it, Mythica thought to herself as she witnessed Mercy persistently banging on their bedroom door rather hard. She knew for a fact the doors were locked and unlocked during their bedtime and when it was time to get up. She then heard the sound of rushing feet heading right for their room, causing Mercy to step back to allow two of the nurses who were caring for them to step in.

One nurse, who wore a blue gown with a white background, looked at Mythica holding a huge pillow over her head and ears. She empathically asked, "How long has she been like this?"

"I don't know. What time is it?" Mythica asked.

"You're just in time to take her away. And the clock on our windowsill isn't working."

The other nurse checked her watch. "It's a quarter to eight o'clock."

Great. Just my luck. She's been screaming for an hour, Mythica thought to herself after taking a guess. *I know I ain't gonna get any sleep tonight.*

"I had a terrible dream," Mercy repeated.

The nurses looked at Mythica, puzzled. She nodded as she began sucking her cheeks in, giving off a hint it was a pain to tell them. This was what had been going on for an hour as she was climbing in to hit the sack. "She says there are two cats and a princess coming. They're looking for crystals to restore her kingdom. These visitors who are coming here are incredibly dangerous."

The two nurses seemed to laugh at this, but the two girls did not to see the humor. They regained their composure.

The head nurse then said, "It's just a dream. There is no princess. I don't believe a word of it."

"But what about the crystals? Surely they exist." Mercy continued with her worrywart ways.

"And what about the ruckus you have caused every night? You always end up waking everyone inside the entire facility every hour that goes by after every nightmare you have with your ear-bleeding screaming. Do you think that's fair to us at all?"

"But I'm just trying to warn you about the danger," Mercy said in a whiny tone. "I was trying to be helpful."

"There is no danger, Mercy," the head nurse continued. She was starting to become annoyed for having to tell her this a second time. She was now thinking they should have the girls sleep in separate rooms. However, she decided it was best to refrain from the idea. She then sat down on Mercy's bed, lending a hand of comfort by placing it on the girl's right shoulder.

Mercy shuddered at the head nurse's touch. She noticed and asked, "Are my hands cold?"

"Yes, a little," Mercy said while trying to stop her teeth from chattering.

"Tell me about it. That's another issue," Mythica said as she rubbed her arms. "It's cold inside this room. I wish I had control over the building's thermostat. Then I'd make it more comfortable, about above 70."

The second nurse turned to face Mythica, ignoring her complaint about the room temperature. "And as for you, how are you feeling after the electroconvulsive therapy?"

"Sick to my stomach about being here," Mythica admitted. "Does that answer your question?" She then rolled over to her side to stare at the white wall behind her as she heard Mercy once again plead that they give a warning to the other residents of the asylum.

"I need to tell the other patients my dream. They need to be warned."

The assistant nurse smiled real fake and said, "Excuse me for a second, Mercy." She went over to the head nurse. "May I speak to you for a minute in the hallway?"

Reading the dark eyes of her assistant, the head nurse nodded. They both stepped out into the corridor. She whispered something about paranoia and how Mercy needed to be electrocuted. It was about the only other option they had, considering she had not dropped it. And telling her it was just a dream and that it was not real wasn't working. The two nurses began to step inside.

Mythica then heard the dark-eyed one say, "Mercy, why don't we take a walk?"

"A walk? It's dark outside."

"I know. However, I think you need one. Come with me and my assistant."

Mercy got up from her bed and followed the two nurses out the door.

Mythica mouthed the words to them as they were shutting the door, "Thank you."

The nurse assistant nodded. "You're welcome. I will allow you to go to sleep. Have a nice night." She then closed the door and headed straight down the hall, joining the head nurse and Mercy.

*****

Sori, who was their next-door neighbor, still remained inside her cottage. Lying on her bed, she breathed a sigh of relief. Finally, silence had come. She removed the pillow from her head, sat up, and peered out her bedroom window. And then she looked around the room. Her eyes then stopped to gaze upon a few of her belongings. She kept a few of her favorite things on a special shelf high above her bed. However, one of them was missing. She had forgotten about her most prized possession: Emme, her stuffed troll! She named it Emme as a child, after her great-grandmother, when she first came to the Land of Lost Luggage. It was sometime before the Toaster-Fire War had broken out among the lands.

The Toaster-Fire War went down with the history behind the island. There are pictures hanging out in the hallway of her house depicting that toasters had once been living spiritual beings around the area before becoming inanimate objects.

The toasters were the ones who had built a huge mud pyramid around a river called the Mobile Bay, where you could catch a ride on the Motorola MicroTAC ran by a herd of dragon-monkeys.

Dragon-monkeys are creatures that have a squirrel-monkey body, dragon wings, and teeny dragon horns upon their heads. You can find them all over the Land of the Lost Luggage, although it's complicated to catch one and keep it as a pet. Dragon-monkeys are very shy and can be incredibly territorial when threatened by people who have set traps for them. They are trapped for their fur and parts.

Male dragon-monkeys were often caught and weren't as threatening. But if you caught a female dragon-monkey, do not mess with her! Set her free. Also, if you spot her nest anywhere among the trees or land, move away and get away from it as far as possible unless you want to lose a finger. You've been warned that mother dragon-monkeys are highly protective of their young.

Thank God I didn't lose a finger, Sori thought to herself as she recalled one person who had. She thought back to her half brother, who was stupid enough to set traps for the dragon-monkeys. It cost him his trigger finger and thumb when he had just gone hunting with a gun. She warned him not to do that because he might get punished for it harshly. She had been right.

Sori got up and went back out to the front porch. That was when she noticed something strange under the lamppost that marked off her streets as part of the swamp. She could see a dark figure in the gleam of the moonlight. He was holding a knife.

Sori rubbed her eyes a little, and as she did, the dark figure disappeared. *It must've been my imagination*, she thought.

It didn't take long for her to be interrupted once more—this time by a sudden blast of gunfire that came from behind her home. She looked to the right, and she could see her grandmother coming from around the house. She was running after a bug that went flying by. Sori's grandmother was a woman who was as old as a witch.

"Come back here, you nasty little fly!" Then Sori heard her grandmother say, "I have something to share with you."

More gunshots were fired, followed by holes being blown through their kitchen windows. The shattering glass caused Sori to wince as unpleasant images came into her mind.

"You know you don't have to waste your time chasing and shooting that pesky little fly with a gun, Grandma," Sori said, getting tired of this shenanigan. "There's something I know that kills flies. It's called a flyswatter."

Sori's grandmother snarled as she looked at her granddaughter standing on the porch. "You shouldn't be out of bed."

"Grandma, I have to get myself used to using this crutch," Sori explained to the old woman who raised her after her mother died from a sickness after birthing her. "I'll be using it for a while."

Her grandmother sighed. "Fine. Just stay away from the swamp and lake. I don't want any more of those crocs taking a bite out of you again."

"No worries," Sori said. "I haven't the slightest interest in going near the lake. Oh, and Nickel has taken our boat for a joy ride."

"Third time this week," her grandmother mumbled as she began to go back into the house. She was exhausted from chasing and shooting her gun off at the fly, which was nowhere to be found. "Tell Mr. Redners, when he's finished with the boat, he leaves it by the pier."

"He knows, mum-mum," Sori said, using her grandmother's nickname, which she and the rest of her family had been using to gain the old woman's attention. It didn't take long for the sound of the sirens from downtown to go off.

Sori took a quick glance at the beautiful, small, quiet town below them. She could see, not too far off, the captain of the guard along with a few horses beginning to gallop in the northern direction.

Nickel, however, was still at the lake doing his fishing, and he was clasping his hands over his sensitive ears. His eyes and face seemed irritated, for they had zero tolerance for the noise coming from the tall towers that watched over their town. A bright light flashed, blinding Sori as she stood not too far from the rest of her community.

Sori had blinked her eyes twice, allowing them to adjust, as a camper bus came driving alongside a huge ship that sailed on the ocean next to them. These passed the bridge entrance to the Land of the Lost Luggage, which was connected to the town, and stopped at the trading post.

"Who is that down there?" Sori questioned her grandmother.

"I don't know, but they better not come looking for me," Sori's grandmother said. "You know I dislike outsiders and strangers that aren't part of our town."

"*My twin bro is home!*" shouted Nickel at the top of his lungs. "*I have seen him!*"

Nickel came rowing back to the shore, making Sori and her grandmother pleased he was returning with the boat he borrowed from them. He tied the boat to the pier again, just the way he had found it, before hopping out and rushing off to meet up with his twin, who was coming from the ships on the dock. He came to a halt with Sori grabbing him by the shirt, slowing him down.

He turned to look at her. "Sori, can you let go? I have to meet up with my bro." He could see Sori was still holding on to him. She had a flat expression as she continued to hold on to him. Nickel looked at her deeply with his green-blue eyes, which were like ice cubes. "What?"

"You're supposed to be in the asylum," Sori said again. "Your brother would be disappointed to see you running loose."

"So what? It wasn't my fault," Nickel began, thinking back to how he escaped.

This was partly true. The two nurses were so incredibly busy dealing with Mercy and her episode that they barely noticed him sneaking out the door.

"But wait. You have forgotten what you were placed inside the asylum for. You threw a rock at one of our churches, breaking a window belonging to our Lord. You got yourself sent there for rage issues," Sori revealed.

"Oh, I don't care about the opinions of others, and neither should you," Nickel said. "Now let me go and see my brother."

"Fine," Sori said as she let him go. "Learn the hard way."

"Aren't you coming with me?"

"Sori isn't going anywhere, Nickel," revealed Sori's grandmother. "She is strictly on bed rest."

A car came up the hillside leading to their little driveway made of sand and dirt. Usually, horses would be trotting up and be tied out in front of Sori's grandmother's little house, but this time, it was a car.

Sori could recognize the driver anywhere. The man turned the van off and opened his car door. He had a straw hat on to block the sunshine from his sensitive eyes, which were the same as Sori's—a sparkling gemstone-green. However, his eyes were not dark enough to be an emerald-green, and his hat couldn't hide the goofy smile he had on his face. He was preparing to carry the groceries from the car into the house.

Sori's grandmother called out to him, "Need help, Joseph?"

Terkina feared for him carrying the groceries by himself, especially with it being hot out. She feared he would end up getting a stroke.

"Yes, Terkina," Joseph said as he began to gather the bags from behind him. Just a few of them though; he couldn't carry them all.

"Would you like me to help?" Sori asked.

"No. You go rest, Sori," replied Terkina as she got down from the porch and headed over to the van to grab a few of the grocery bags. "You need it."

Sori went back into the house as Terkina assisted her father with the groceries. They came into the house, and to her father's horror, he could see the kitchen windows shot up with holes in the glass. He could see the .33 on the counter as evidence that hadn't been erased from the scene.

"What happened to the windows?" Joseph asked.

Sori came into the room. "Don't you know, Dad? Grandma was shooting at a fly again."

Joseph rolled his eyes at Terkina. "We have a flyswatter, Mom, hanging up inside the snack cabinet over there. Why didn't you use it?"

"I prefer to go with the extremes," Terkina said simply as she narrowed her eyes, which were beaming, at her son. "The extreme of doing things my way."

Joseph sighed. "Whatever. Why don't you put the groceries away?" He began to walk toward the door when he heard Terkina calling to him.

"Wait, a minute. Where are you going?"

"Back into town. I'm going to the dock to meet and greet our new guests who have followed the other followers of Lucifer straight to our island," Joseph said.

"Can I come, Dad?" Sori asked. "I would love to check out these strangers too."

Joseph looked at Terkina inquiringly. She shrugged her shoulders. It must be really up to him to decide if he would give permission to Sori to travel with him along the coastline.

"I don't see why not," Joseph said, scratching his chin as he adjusted his straw hat upon his head. He heard a cheerful high-pitched cry from his daughter.

"Thank you! Thank you! Thank you!" Sori said, hugging Joseph, which made him put his arms around her.

"You're welcome," Joseph said. "Go out and get inside the car."

Sori left the house, allowing Joseph and Terkina to have time alone inside the kitchen to speak to each other. Terkina then said to Joseph, "You really spoil her, you know that?"

"This isn't spoiling," Joseph explained. "It's called getting your daughter out of the house."

"Do you think she'll be all right going into town? Especially after her mother, years ago…you know." Terkina could see it pained her son to even speak of his second wife's passing. Sori's mother wandered the streets one rainy night looking for him, and she ended up catching an incurable lung infection, which was serious due to his wife having heart and lung complications. Luckily, she was found by some of the townsfolk, and they had taken her into a warm and dry sanctuary somewhere, where she safely gave birth to Sori and died.

Joseph hadn't forgotten the phone call he received. They had recognized his wife when she was walking the rainy streets alone. After she was laid to rest, the doctors and townsfolk had greatly feared Sori would contract it and die as well. But none of that happened. It was a miracle Sori turned out to be a healthy and strong child, and she had grown into a perfectly beautiful young lady—so beautiful, it pained her father sometimes because of how she resembled her mother.

Joseph, Terkina, and Sori's older half brother, Jerry, had all gone into town to get her as the townsfolk began to make funeral arrangements for Sori's mother. During the arrangements, Jerry had taken Sori home to his mother, who gave her the care the girl needed and really appreciated for the past fourteen years of her life.

"Might as well get going to the trading post," Joseph said after Terkina had finished putting away the groceries he had brought.

"Yeah, I need to get some traps, Dad," Jerry said. "I'm sure the trading post will have enough traps in order for me too."

"What did I say about hunting dragon-monkeys?" Joseph questioned his son.

"It's not for dragon-monkeys, Dad. I want to trap and catch coons around the woods. If there are any left." Jerry glanced down at his left hand, which bore the lingering consequences for his actions. He wore a black glove over where his trigger finger and thumb had once been.

"You may hunt coons. But please, Jerry. No hunting dragon-monkeys," Terkina reminded him.

Jerry rolled his eyes. "Whatever." And he headed out to the car, where he could see Sori had already taken the front seat. He shook his head and got into the back seat right behind the driver.

Joseph soon came out after laughing and talking with Terkina for a little while.

"All right. Don't be a stranger to the newcomers. Be sure to greet them with respect," Terkina said as she watched Joseph go around the truck and open the driver's door.

"I will. Wish us luck," Joseph said as he hopped into the driver's seat and closed the door. He began to start the engine, making the kids anticipate their expedition meeting the new outsiders in town. He could see Nickel walking down toward the docks. "You want to ride with us, Nickel? It's faster."

Nickel glanced up from looking at his feet and faced Joseph. He then said, "No, sir. I prefer to walk. Could use the exercise."

"Suit yourself." Joseph drove on.

Chapter 13

Sorphina faced the head of the stern part of the ship. She could feel the cool misty air through her yellow fur. It made her feel rather peppy as it blew on through. She stared out at the landmass ahead of them. "What do you think, Zacky?" She turned to face the boy, who remained standing behind her on the dock.

Zack was busy scratching behind his neck as he took a quick glance over his shoulder at what he had left behind. He was feeling smitten. So smitten, in fact, that he didn't hear Sorphina. He kept on thinking repeatedly about Princess Lauren and how attractive she was. He then heard her call his name again.

"Zack," Sorphina repeated.

He snapped out of it. "What, Foxy?"

Sorphina refrained from reacting toward the term *foxy*. She hated it when he called her Foxy. She let it go and asked again, "What do you think of being home? It feels good, doesn't it?"

Zack thought quickly. "It's fine. I love viewing our landmass all burned up."

*****

Pumpkin could see a rusty old sign with lights blinking that said Roasty-Toasty Traders as he peeked through his open driver's window and pulled the Boot-Hoot into the parking lot. It came to a halt, bringing them to the Land of the Lost Luggage.

Princess Lauren, who remained sitting in the front passenger seat, couldn't believe what her enormous brown eyes were viewing. All over, there was no sign of life—nothing except darkness and death all over. There were no plants, no food, and the buildings were all run-down and abandoned. It was kind of similar to an old ghost town no one visits. Could this area be haunted?

"This is disturbing," Lauren said, not realizing she was speaking her thoughts out loud.

"What's disturbing about it?" Pumpkin asked, getting a sense the princess was afraid of this spooky town. "We cannot skip this town, Lauren. We must go through here."

"I know we cannot skip it," Lauren said. "But there is something about this land. It just throws me off. It makes me want to not exit the Boot-Hoot and stay here."

"Oh, don't be silly, Lauren," Pumpkin said after placing the Boot-Hoot in park. He then turned to his brother. "Tigger, please find a suit for Princess Lauren to wear around the area. It's for her safety. The next crystal is around here somewhere. Remember when we were back at Bad-Mouther's Brook? We had discovered three bottles holding black liquid belonging to a Georgia Pomegranate and Peggy Entwistle. We have to seek these two women out. They reside around this burned-up wasteland."

Suit? What does Pumpkin mean? Lauren could then hear Tigger heading over to a closet in the back of the Boot-Hoot. He opened its door, revealing a couple of suits hanging up and ready for astronauts to wear. He took one out. It was about Lauren's size—a small blue one.

Why in the world would she need a suit made for an astronaut? They had oxygen around here. They weren't in outer space or on some strange desolate planet. "What is that?" Lauren asked.

"A suit for you," Tigger replied, handing it to her. "You'll need it during our visit here at the Land of the Lost Luggage. It'll protect you from the sun's rays on this island, which will give you heat rashes, sunburn, or stroke."

"Sunrays?" Lauren looked at the land outside. The sun was shining high in the sky. These cats had to be kidding her. She thought of something else. "What about the usage of sunscreen? Wouldn't it be easier than having me wear a suit all day?"

"No, a suit is better. It has an air-conditioner built inside too," Pumpkin revealed. "I have designed these suits in case we have someone who burns easily."

"We have an umbrella," Tigger said, thinking about the umbrella they had in the closet. If Princess Lauren didn't want to wear the suit, he could hold an umbrella and follow her around with it.

Lauren looked at the umbrella. She then said, "Never mind. I'll wear the suit."

Lauren unzipped the back zipper after unscrewing the helmet. She then stepped in, preparing herself.

Pumpkin grabbed his cowboy hat from the closet and walked into the kitchen to get other things they might need.

Sighing, Lauren zipped up as she peered outside at the Land of the Lost Luggage.

The End

About the Author

Lauren Andrea Bischoff is a young woman from Bucks County, Pennsylvania. Lauren was diagnosed with autism at seven years old and has worked hard to overcome challenges. As a young girl, she always enjoyed writing stories and poems and dreamed of being an author. The Knowledge Crystals is Lauren's first published work. Lauren has a love for all animals. The characters are from some of Lauren's experiences as well as from her vivid imagination. She worked on this book for several years and wrote several different versions. This is her final vision.